P9-CRO-747

When She Was Queen

Also by MG Vassanji

The In-Between World of Vikram Lall

Amriika

The Book of Secrets

No New Land

Uhuru Street

The Gunny Sack

When She Was Queen

MG VASSANJI

DOUBLEDAY CANADA

Doubleday Canada and colophon are trademarks.

Library and Archives Canada Cataloguing in Publication
Vassanji, M. G.
    When she was queen / M.G. Vassanji.
ISBN 0-385-66176-2
    I. Title.
PS8593.A87W44 2005   C813'.54   C2005-904190-0

Jacket images: (woman on card) csaimages.com, (cards) © Royalty-
    Free/CORBIS, (background) © Rykoff Collection/CORBIS
Jacket and text design: Kelly Hill
Printed and bound in the USA

Published in Canada by
Doubleday Canada, a division of
Random House of Canada Limited

Visit Random House of Canada Limited's website: www.randomhouse.ca

BVG   10   9   8   7   6   5   4   3   2   1

For Harish and Alka

Contents

When She Was Queen

My father lost my mother one evening in a final round of gambling at the poker table. I have often tried to recall that moment, its exact details of scene and mood, though I was not present there, could not have been. I was, if you will, the contingent phenomenon, a potential lurking in the unholy fug of a revelrous night spun out of control. My father's gesture was not the nail-biting one of a compulsive gambler who, having lost

all, imagines with diseased mind he will redeem himself
with just that one hand that Lady Luck, his kismet, was
bound to throw his way. Nor was there an epic dimension
to that fateful moment—ancient enemy seeking ultimate
revenge—castration in public. My father was unusual in
many ways; but he was also a simple innkeeper, who succumbed in an instant to one gigantic temptation. He had
already won a few hundred shillings that night, not a tri-
fling sum for him. But then, in all the whimsical naivety
of his nature he let his good sense abandon him. He saw
a miraculous vision of more, he desired it to distraction.
On the table for him to win was a palatial lakeside residence, which turned Mother heartbreakingly wistful and
envious every time she set her eyes on it, and which he
could never hope to provide her in a hundred years with
his wages. When John Chacha, known otherwise as the
Asian King of Kisumu, declared magnanimously, "I am
ready to bid what is dearest to me, this alishaan mansion—there, you have a chance to wipe me out and move
in with your lovely wife into my castle—" Father said,
"Don't I only wish I had something of value to match
your bid."

John Chacha, with his impressive, oversized head
and abundant white mane, beamed at my father across
the table.

"You have," he said. "You have exactly such a thing."

The few people standing around the table followed
the big man's wolfish leer and smiled in nervous anticipation. And my fair and beautiful mother, with her
stylishly modern, short brown hair and shimmering
olive-green sari, on whom that eye fell as she stood

watching behind her red-faced husband: Why did she choose to remain silent?

I have gleaned this story from whatever my mother Shirin, and my two elder sisters Razia and Habibeh, who were then seven and nine years old, have relinquished to my queries. We all live in Toronto now, far from Kisumu by Lake Victoria, and my father Rashid has been dead twenty years. Let us say that over the years enough allusion to that eventful night had flown past me, uncomprehended, that finally I decided to uncover all the mystery surrounding it.

In the mid-1960s my family were settled in Kisumu, down from the western ridge of the Great Rift Valley, in the cosy equatorial embrace of the Lake Victoria shoreline. It was soon after the independence of Kenya, life in this new sunshine was freer and livelier than it had ever been before; the Indians were emerging from the former mingy, scrappy existence of their neighbourhoods. There was money around, and there was life to be lived. I recall a happy childhood from those days, and legends about the hardships and migrations of a distant past. My father Rashid, who had tried his hand as a salesman at a hunting store in Nairobi, as a safari rally driver and navigator, and as manager of a timber mill and later a tea plantation, had been enticed when the plantation was sold by its owners to manage one Rose Hotel in Kisumu. Rashid Jafar was an outsider in Kisumu, but because of having worked with Europeans and acquired certain mannerisms and habits as a result, and due to his brush with glory when he and his co-driver came close to beating the Swedish aces Erikson and Erikson in the East African Safari rally (their Peugeot

404 overturned on the home stretch outside Nairobi), he was welcomed by the rich Asians of that town.

Every Friday night a certain rambunctious group among this elite would meet at the Rose Hotel for a late dinner from its renowned menu. The kitchen at the Rose was famous from Nairobi to Kampala for its rich spicy dishes—the chicken tikka, the lamb biryani, the coconut and coriander fish, and the naans and parathas; tourist handbooks raved about its tantalizing aromas and rich tastes, and airline pilots were known to hitch rides with each other to eat there. This glory of the Rose was a creation of my father.

He would say his hero was the famous explorer Henry Morton Stanley—whose name was more apt to draw scorn and contempt in independent East Africa for his reputed cruelty, but what Rashid admired about that American was his pure gumption, the fact that he, a foreigner, simply arrived on the scene one day and started up the Congo River on foot and on boat and wound up ultimately not far from our town in the heart of the continent. Rashid's spirit was not of the outdoors type, but he too was a mover, a migrant. Kisumu, he would say, was his final stop.

I loved him. There was never a time when, if you put your hand in his jacket pocket, you would not come out with a Trebor or Bluebird candy, a box of Smarties, a cylinder of Rolo chocolate, a packet of Pez awaiting your grasping child's hand. Mother said he had a hole in his pocket, but for me that pocket was Ali Baba's cave. John Chacha would tell him, Your staff eats better than me.

I recall a man slim of build, not very tall, and rather dark, with a narrow face and sparse hair; the face smelling deliciously of Old Spice aftershave and stale cigarette. He had a peculiar habit, when posed to listen to anyone, of facing away, with a tilt of the head downward, lending them his ear, so to speak. Always in a light grey or blue suit, he could be found at the hotel reception, or in the kitchen, or striding along a corridor somewhere in between those two destinations; in the evenings he sat in the bar or the dining room among his patrons. Mother supervised housekeeping and shopping for the kitchen.

My father—so I must call him, still—could talk the ears off someone when he was inclined to, and this would usually be a hotel guest, who had time on his hands and loose change for a beer and the slot machines and would say to him, Have one on me, Mr. Jafar, and my father would reply, No, no, it's on me, what are you having, and soon he would be rattling on about his life, until a messenger would come to fetch him for an urgent phone call, or an emergency in the kitchen, and the guest would sit back with relief and pick up his mug.

You know, what may seem the most casual or trivial of events can turn out to change your life, my father would begin when asked about how he entered the hotel business.

The old English couple who had owned the Burton Tea Estates near Kericho were packing to leave, and the new owner, a minister in the new Kenya government, had already given my father his marching orders. It was around eleven on a cool misty morning in the hills, father out in the veranda of his bungalow having tea and sandwiches—his was a wonderfully relaxed plantation lifestyle in the colonial mode, except that his family were out in Nairobi and he would get lonely. The guard at the gate came and knocked on his screen door, saying, "Bwana, there's this mister here, an Indian whose car has broken down on the road."

A tall man in a tropical suit, wearing sunglasses, stepped in, followed by two children, a boy of six and a girl of nine.

"John Karmally," said the man, "from Kisumu. How are you? I believe a gasket is blown."

He removed the shades, cast an eye around to inspect the premises. The veranda had an old table and chair, a prominent radio, and above that on the wall a calender bearing the picture of the goddess Lakshmi.

My father bade the visitor sit, noted his oversized head and white mane, though he wasn't much older. He ordered more tea, and a mechanic was dispatched with Mr. Karmally's chauffeur to bring the car back to the estate where it could be seen to.

John Chacha, as we would come to know the man, stayed the day. My father, showing him the hospitality and carefree manner that were his mark, took his visitor to the town and introduced him to the local Indian merchants. John Chacha had a delightful stay, spending the night with an acquaintance. And by the next morning, when he was about to set off for Nairobi, having learned of my father's current predicament, he offered him a job as manager of the Rose Hotel in Kisumu.

*

My mother was a stunningly beautiful woman, with a bearing suggestive of quiet dignity and arrogance. In the evening she preferred to come out in a sari, which fell as naturally down her body as the plume of a bird; thus attired, when she made her presence known in a room, it was as if the lighting had suddenly altered. Even as a child I was aware of her brilliance when she was dressed and all made up. The ample closet which our hotel home could afford her was a dizzying riot of colours and odours, among which I would sometimes go and hide, to nurse my wounds. But I recall her also in a blue and black kitenge suit with matching headgear, at a Rose Hotel ball to celebrate our independence day anniversary, when the Area Commissioner and the Mayor were among the guests, this being our Indian way to ingratiate ourselves with prickly African politicians. Even now, as I walk with her along Don Mills Road and sit on the lawn outside the Science Centre, as she weakly clutches at my arm and reminds me that she is not as young as I, her beauty and shape have not deserted her. Her face is more drawn but makes her all the more striking, the body is frail but still betrays the shape beneath the sari, and those discerning, curious looks will inevitably land upon her.

I was the youngest of her children and by far, from what I observed myself and of which I have always been reminded, the closest to her. My two sisters were brought up with the assistance of ayahs. But I demanded so much from her, by my frailty and being the youngest, and she was willing to give so much, that apparently all the credit for her later reserve falls upon me. This may only be sibling rivalry talking. I do know for certain that I needed her a lot as a child, her close presence was a comfort that I often craved.

She was the eldest girl in a modest household. Her own parents had died and she lived with her mother's sister. Some of her younger cousins had already married, and as often happened in such cases—an orphaned girl with diminished prospects—she was given away a little too easily. My father was a drifting salesman in Nairobi; smoked; drank a bit. He would make a living but would never be a rich man. But, as the saying went, even half a husband, a one-eyed one or a lame one, for example, was better than none at all. My father's handicaps were hardly so serious; and besides, the two families were distantly acquainted.

Imagine, she says. A man, his trousers tucked inside his wellingtons, wearing a thick sweater, then a greatcoat on top, setting off on a horse early at dawn, into the mist-strewn forest of the Elburgon Hills, to mark out trees for the day's cutting. His keys, tied to his belt, tinkling softly in the half dark. This was during the years when he managed a sawmill. Once he met a gang of freedom fighters returning from a raid and promised to bring them a package of corned beef and a couple of old bicycle pumps the next morning, which he did. He could have been hanged for that. Or imagine someone who spends all his savings to enter a safari rally in Nairobi and nearly wins. Nearly; your father was not an out-and-out winner, that was never his style.

She catches my eye; the spot of pink on her cheeks deepens a shade, and I look away from my mother.

In Kisumu, she says, your father and I seemed finally to be settling down.

The "Johnnies" ruled Kisumu, if to rule meant to be the envy of the town and to set the trend for the other rich Indians to follow; if it meant to possess enough wealth that all kinds of influence and licence were a phone call away. They were called the Johnnies because of their wildly extravagant ways and because the most prominent among them had adopted the English name John. On Friday nights they hit the town, together with their wives, stopping off finally at the Rose. My father Rashid supplied their victuals and libations, and the gambling tables; and as the night wore on, and their tired wives retired to one corner of the hotel to sit, wait, and chat, he turned a blind eye to their sins, as one or two of them began hunting the bar for a bit of exotic flesh on the side, a beautiful African girl or a down-on-her-luck European, and gave the nod for a room to be made available. Rashid was not one of the Johnnies, he was an employee; but he was at home with Western customs more than these rich merchants who'd made their money in all sorts of ways, and so they liked to have him around. He introduced them to airline pilots and stewardesses on their nightly layovers, the occasional tourist, and once the famous Dr. Leakey passing through with part of a human cranium in his briefcase. He gave them the taste for a good martini, he introduced them to the slick Manhattan, the Nairobi punch, the exclusive Dodoma wine, of which, according to him, a few hundred bottles were prepared with devotion every year by a mission in central Tanzania that very few knew about.

In addition to John Chacha, the group included Ambalal, a gregarious man with a freckled face, flaming red curly hair, and the red mouth of the habitual paan-chewer; the quiet, cadaver-like Hassam Mukhi, who wore yellow cotton suits and always seemed quite lost; the diminutive, well-mannered Dr. Patel, who was never without a necktie; the tall and handsome Dr. Singh, the medical expert of last resort and only cancer specialist in town.

Every eight weeks or so, on a Saturday night, there would be the anticipated "party" at one of the better homes. This was a family event; children were seen in hordes, servants packed the kitchen, the men and women mingled happily and domestically together. The occasional birthday or Eid or Diwali was remembered and celebrated with due fanfare. Drinks flowed, the women making a show of sophistication in this privacy, clinking glasses of tepid baby cham; there was the bawdy joke or two related loudly for the pleasure of all; there was a gaming table for the compulsive gamblers.

On the fateful evening that would become the obsessive and dark centre of my existence, the party was at John Chacha's. Mother and Father drove down from the hotel with their two daughters in their ancient green Morris. On the way, as Mother always demanded during such visits, they passed the former British properties of the Lavington Avenue area—dreamy tree-shaded bungalows behind large lots, their French or bay windows emitting a cosy warm light into the thick darkness—the sights of which never failed to provoke wistful sighs from her and consequent pangs of male guilt in him.

Their drive took them uphill, next to the lakeshore, and John Chacha's was the last house on a broad cul-de-sac at the edge of a cliff, the road leading straight into the driveway and back. Behind it, a few hundred feet below, lay Lake Victoria. Sometimes, through the back windows, the meagre lights of one of the handful of passenger ships which plied the lake would be visible, in a background of pitch blackness. The house itself was likened to an ocean liner, due to its size and location. It had a white exterior, with teak doors and windows, the latter equipped with louvred shutters. The gravelled driveway, bordered with gleaming white flagstones, led straight up to a grand portico supported on two columns. I see my father park his modest conveyance among the others', the four of them get out, my sisters scampering up ahead of them to the door, from behind which come the sounds of party, men's guffaws, women's peals; lights on in every window. The couple enter, mingle in the crowd, the door closes.

Father was never fazed by wealth; he accepted it as a matter of course that some people were born into it, others acquired it through a combination of cleverness and sleaze, and the rest didn't have it. He had no regrets about his life, he would tell his wife, he would never have become a businessman. She thought he excused himself a little too easily. What made our family acceptable in such a group was his manner, and her beauty and style.

The inside of the house was appointed with lush drapes and carpets, heavy dark wood furniture of the European style; there were knick-knacks collected from every part of the world, paintings and curios, some marked with names of foreign cities, which the children would stare long at, imagining exotic places. Overseeing all the goings-on in the vast drawing room were two large framed photographs of John Chacha's parents on a wall, his father urbane in a typical round turban and a suit, tricorn white handkerchief sticking out from his breast pocket, his mother with her head covered in the Gujarati-style pachedi, nose stud glinting, looking very ancient and grim. The old man had made his money in cashews and jam.

It was the eve of John Chacha's wife Khanoo Chachi's departure for Mombasa to visit her family. Both children would go with her. Some of the guests had brought presents for her, there were parcels to take for relations. There was consequently a certain amount of nervous excitement in the air that night. The journey would be by train, taking two days, from the lake up to the highest station in Kenya, close to where father had worked in a sawmill, then down via Nairobi to the coast. Khanoo Chachi reminded all to look after her husband in her absence, and they assured her not to worry, they would do so and make sure he kept out of mischief. Mother knew all the stations on the line and went over them with Khanoo Chachi. Her father had worked on the railways—as an engineer, she always insisted; as a guard, my father would protest with equal force. His own father had been a ticket collector.

Toward the middle of the proceedings, John Chacha, seated by himself with a drink at the card table, was served a brand new pack, which he stripped open, saying, "Who'll make a foursome with me?"

"I don't mind winning some," Dr. Patel muttered, coming over with a twinkle in his eyes.

"Or losing some, Patel, welcome."

Ambalal came rolling over, whisky in one hand, soda in the other. "Just a few rounds, John, last time you took the pants off me."

Just then Father passed by.

"Eh, Rashid, just the chap. Come and join us," John Chacha beckoned him over.

"Let's strip the chap naked," Ambalal whispered with a snicker.

"Yes, let's," said Patel quietly.

Father hesitated. Ambalal turned on his wheedling voice. "Arré, come neh, be a sport. Enough of chatting up the women. Join the men now. It's time we rub John's nose in the dirt."

Father took a seat, and started winning.

As the pile of chips beside him started growing, the wives and other guests gathered around to watch. John Chacha was losing the most, and he had become tense and curt. He was not a good loser. Ambalal was his chirpy self, though far from a winner. Dr. Patel was a few chips down at most. Mother stood quietly behind Father, looking serene. Beside her loomed Dr. Singh next to the African intern he had brought with him to the party. It was about time to break up and leave, only the cue to do so awaited the initiative. It was then that John Chacha made his offer, bidding his palatial residence.

Khanoo Chachi gave a gasp, saying, "You can't!"

Her husband raised a hand to quiet her, throwing her a sharp look, and said: "I have just done so." He smiled expansively at the players round the table, his edginess suddenly gone.

"Don't I only wish I had something of value to bid against that," Father said, sounding regretful.

John Chacha beamed at him. "You have! If I have a palace, you have the Queen of Kisumu! You can do better than the Pandavas, surely."

The reference was to the five Pandava brothers of mythology, who gambled away their wife in a game of dice.

"Arré what is he saying, this man," Khanoo Chachi said in despair. "Have some shame, for God's sake." She started crying. She was an emotional, uncomplicated and kind woman, admired and pitied for enduring the trial that was her marriage.

"Bid her," said the undeterred John Chacha to my father, "and if you win, this alishaan mansion, this Taj Mahal of Lake Province"—he made a gesture to indicate all its grandeur—"is yours for you and your Mumtaz to move into. If not. . . ."

"If not?"

"If not, she's mine for a night."

There was laughter from the spectators.

"So you think," Father replied, with pluck. "I'll beat you this time, Johnny-boy. All right, my wife on the table." He threw a quick look at my mother, who stood behind him smiling.

"Can they do this?" the African intern asked Dr. Singh.

"It's only a joke," someone said beside them and chortled with nervous excitement. It was Dr. Patel's wife. The haughty Dr. Singh threw her a look of scorn.

The intern turned away with a look of disgust, then turned back again to watch the hand played out.

Father lost. He got up, his face flushed.

Dr. Singh and his friend were the first to leave, then all the others started packing up their children and heading for the door. It was a typical leave-taking, with many best wishes and reminders to meet again. Khanoo Chachi had been subdued by the women telling her it was all a joke, and men will be men, John especially. John Chacha stood beside her next to the door, equally subdued and polite in a drunken way. They shook hands with my father, did pranams to my mother. Ambalal and his wife Moti and their three children came out with Mother and Father, and as they separated in the driveway, Ambalal said to Father, "Well, you lost your wife. You have to watch this Johnny, he pulls the pants off you if you give him the chance."

When they reached home, my mother and father fought.

"So you simply gambled me away. Like this," she snapped her fingers. "What did you think of me?"

"I was a fool, darling, but it was for you that I was tempted!"

"And so you sold away my dignity."

"You could have stopped me! You could have objected! You *allowed* it!"

"We were all watching *you* to see what you would do! You accepted an insult to your wife! You *sold* me away! Well, if my husband thinks me dispensable enough a commodity—"

"We were all a bit tipsy," Father said desperately.

"John especially. I'll call him tomorrow, tell him it was all a joke. He should apologize. Come on, I am sorry . . ."

The next morning he called up John. "I say, my wife's a bit upset—that joke went a bit too far and I think—"

"You know I don't joke when I gamble and when I do business."

"But this time you joked, and I think—"

"I didn't joke. I bid my house fair and square, with all my honour at stake, and I take it that you too bid fairly. I could have lost, and you would have won my house. As it stands, I won."

"What do you mean?"

"I won your wife for a night, Rashid. Tonight I'll send a car for her."

The car came, and she strode out to it, dignified as ever, dressed in her finest.

"So, did they?" I ask my two sisters.

On one side of the large deck at Habibeh's Scarborough home, her husband and son barbecue meat and vegetables in an instance of father-son bonding I find quite touching. Teenagers shoot hoops in the distance, at the far end of the backyard, among them the other children of the family. Mother sits out on the lawn, protected by an umbrella, in the company of a new friend she's brought with her today and her other son-in-law. And Habibeh, Razia, and I sit huddled together on the deck, transported by our habitual closeness, which my mother and my two brothers-in-law sometimes find tiresome.

"Did they what," Razia asks, puckering her lips, sending a devilish glance at Habibeh.

"You know what I mean—sleep together," I say, reddening. How the utterly unspeakable finds a voice, given time. My sisters never lost their habit of teasing me mercilessly.

Now they raise their eyebrows at each other. "You have to ask her," says Razia.

"Don't be silly. How can I ask Mother *that*? You must know—was John Chacha my real father? The date fits, doesn't it, more or less?"

I was born nine and a half months after that eventful night, delivered by Caesarian section.

"Sometimes you can't tell," Habibeh says.

All three of us look toward our mother, casually conversing, as composed as ever.

"I thought women could always tell."

"Not always. You should get married," Razia advises.

"What does that have to do with anything?"

Mother lives by herself on Don Mills Road. She is too proud to live with me, which is as well, because I too have my own sense of decorum and privacy. Her one-bedroom flat is dizzying in its plethora of colour and *objets d'art* of the type fashionable in Kenya's Indian homes in the 1960s—copper and batik hangings, Jack-and-Jill and Bo-Peep glass statuettes, Indian dolls that dance; embroidered cushions crowd the chairs, and the air is faintly perfumed. The place has the feel of a shrine. Left alone here, I often tell myself, I would in a few moments rid it of all its clutter and oppressive aura. My father Rashid's picture hangs on a wall next to hers. Both photographs are large and full-length; he looks grey and diminutive in his, she, naturally, bright and stately.

We left Kenya for Toronto a year after the Asians of neighbouring Uganda were expelled by the dictator Idi Amin, in the early seventies. It was a traumatic, uncertain time for the Asians of East Africa. Fearing impending disaster, John Chacha had wound down his business, sold the Rose Hotel, and left Kisumu; my father was again out of a job. Five years after our arrival in Toronto, my father suffered a heart attack. He was taken to hospital and there died from surgical complications. What was remarkable about his death was that we accepted it so readily; there was no great show of grief. Now I realize that this was so because we all knew that a good part of him had already died. He always carried with him the sadness of his humiliation at the gaming table; and then, in Canada, his active life was over, he was in a city that was alien to his nature, where he had nothing to do.

Once a week in the afternoon I come visit my mother, and immediately, for she's ready and waiting for me, we go for a walk along Don Mills Road, by the Science Centre; when the weather is good we sit by the fountain there. How peaceful, she might say, regaining her breath, taking in the scenery. How beautiful this city is. When we return to her apartment she will put on some tea and place savouries before me, and she might probe me on my private life. What happened to that Jane? she will ask. She was so nice; or, That Anita, she turned out no good? Too outspoken, if you ask me. On several occasions, though, through some clever manipulation, I have led her back to the past, in Kisumu, when she was queen. But that night of revelry, when this queen was gambled away, and the following night, its dark aftermath, always prove elusive to my probings of her.

One day, in sheer exasperation, I ask her point-blank: "Tell me about this John Chacha of ours. Was he completely no good? Was he really an evil man, beyond common decency? What was he capable of?"

She eyes me a moment, then speaks quietly: "You listen to your sisters too much. They were all the same, those men. Johnny was no worse than the rest. But he was an arrogant man . . . and he had his good sides too."

It is time to meet the man himself.

John Karmally lives with his wife in Scarborough, not far from Habibeh. Word is that the couple tried living with each of their two sons in Canada, and this is where they've ended up, in an apartment by themselves. As I enter, having made an appointment first, I am taken to the living room by Khanoo Chachi—a diminutive old woman now. They've been watching a Bombay musical, which John Chacha, standing up, puts on low volume. Khanoo Chachi disappears, and I take this to be a meaningful sign.

The room is decorated with choice African motifs. Carvings on display tables, a pair of spears crossed on a wall, a large drum of animal skin, an almost full-size statue of a Masai. John Chacha stands bent and arthritic next to the muscular, upright warrior of gleaming, polished, red wood. Of his previously abundant mane, there remains only a thin strawy patch on the pate.

"How's your mother?" he asks. He has a way of looking from the sides of his eyes, which makes me wonder if he is squint-eyed. There is an intermittent shaking of the head, a symptom of mild Parkinson's, I gather.

"She's well," I reply.

He sits down with a motion of his hand, and I follow suit, across from him.

"And your sisters—they are all right?"

"Yes."

A moment's stillness. Then: "Your father—a pity, he died suddenly. A good man, Rashid."

"Was he my father?" I ask without ado, for I have come determined to take some answer with me.

He looks at me, trying desperately to control a fit of shaking in his upper body. "Your father."

I take it he did not hear me well.

"Rashid, my father—"

"Yes."

"Was he my father, John Chacha?"

He pauses a very brief moment. "It's your mother's business to tell you, isn't it."

How can he be my father? If he were, he would want to claim me, wouldn't he? This man sounds testy, he wants to shrink from me. He knows why I question him, but won't say any more. I would like to ask him, That evening when you sent a car for my mother. . . .

We turn to stare at each other. In my face must be a plea. I'm not sure what to say, how to proceed. But I don't want to leave empty-handed.

"Tell me what's on your mind," he offers, finally.

"You are not my father," I say.

"No. Talk to your mother. I did not dishonour her. It's that night that's on your mind. . . . Your father Rashid and I played a game. It was only a game."

"Rashid is my father, then, as I always thought."

"Talk to your mother. It was a game, as I told you. She left my house unmolested. Dr. Singh, her physician, took her away, when she called him from my house."

She called Dr. Singh to pick her up and not my father.

Dr. Singh, who was my biological father, died in Kisumu in 1978. This was two years before Rashid, whom I think of as my real father, died in Toronto. Of their affair, my mother cannot say much to me. But she has revealed that there was love, indeed passion, between them, and it lasted many years. They wrote letters, she more than he, when she first moved to Canada and suffered acute depression. Her husband knew of the affair and that I was not his real child. When he bid my mother at the poker game that night, he knew that she was not his anyway.

The Girl on the Bicycle

"Are you sure?" exclaims Farida, in disbelief.

"Of course I'm sure." Am I? Yes I am, unbelievable though my story sounds. "I'm positive she did it, right there in front of my eyes."

Anaar Dhalla, imperceptible to anyone but me and one other person, spat at a corpse this morning as it lay in state at a funeral in the foyer of the Main Mosque.

The dead man was from a fairly prominent family back in Dar, though he had had his share of knocks as a new immigrant. He wound up, using his family's money, owning a bicycle factory in the northwest of the city, and more recently was part of a growing investment syndicate and a generous community benefactor.

"I told you I also saw her smiling at the sympathy sitting last night." Crying tears, too, two fat streams rolling down those white cheeks, in the gathering at the back of the mosque after prayers, where friends, relatives, and anyone else who felt like it sat down on the carpet with the widow and family in a gesture of grief sharing.

Anaar, a few persons away on the widow's right, had quite suddenly—and briefly—beamed a sunny smile through her tear-stained face, prompting one rather to think of a rainbow. I found myself with a tiny smile too, recalling that sometimes the funniest thoughts intrude on the gravest of moments, such as this one. There was nothing more to be said about that smile, until that event at the funeral.

At funerals, selected members of the extended family, and friends, come forward in threes to pay their last respects to the dead. (Once upon a time, everyone present, even children, did the same, one by one.) They kneel and join hands on one side of the deceased, brought fresh and glistening in a casket straight from the funeral home, and recite the formula asking forgiveness of sins; on the other side of them sits the mukhi, who grants the forgiveness. I am never completely sure if, at this time, one is craving forgiveness from the dead or on behalf of the dead, but I as mukhi have to sprinkle holy water on him, so I guess it must be the latter. Anaar was one of those selected to come forward for the ceremony, and she took her turn with two other women and knelt by the casket. She had come from work and wore a tan skirt, white blouse, and black waistcoat. A few streaks of red were visible where her shoulder-length wavy hair had been hennaed. I stared perhaps too long at her. It is difficult to keep strictly unworldly when beautiful women kneel in front of you in seductive gravity and grief, and a delicate waft of perfume's just teased your senses. She was third in the row, closer to the corpse's feet, and when the other two women got up after the ceremony, she delayed, then moved up on her knees to peer at the face—as if displaying a special closeness or grief—and spat at it. The act was more like a gesture, but a droplet of spit undeniably flew from her pursed lips onto the embalmed face, landing on the nose. My second, sitting beside me, was the only other person to witness this uncanny scene and looked startled, but I reassured him with a nod, saying, "She only choked. . . ."

"What are you thinking?" Farida asks, after a while.

"Nothing much. Only how time's passed."

We often sit together in the evenings, and when there's nothing much on the tube we muse about various things, among which the past figures often.

"Yes," she agrees, "it has"; and falls into a silent musing of her own.

The thought—or sight—of Anaar never fails to prompt me to recall how I knew her once—at a different time, in another place—as a somewhat sharply featured, fair-skinned girl with a pigtail riding a ladies' bike, the only woman cyclist in the city of my birth, Dar es Salaam.

~

"Your uncle was ever so nice," Anaar said.

"Oh yes?—where did you see him—what happened?" Guli asked, even though Anaar could tell that her friend already knew. Guli's uncle must have told her about the incident, that altercation with the loafers yesterday.

It was late, past six o'clock and close to grey dusk, the menacing maghrab of evil spirits abroad, and she had been returning from drama practice—on Jamhuri Street past the Odeon and on to Uhuru Street on her bicycle. This was an Indian area, she preferred it to the African area behind it, the unpaved streets beyond the Mnazi Moja grounds, which would have taken her on a straighter route home. Not that anything had happened to her in that area, or to anyone she knew. Africans made her nervous—not the older men, in kanzus, whom she respected and called "Mzee" for grandfather, but the younger men, closer to her age; they seemed to laugh and sneer at you as if they didn't care two bits what you said or thought, what your life consisted of. Couple of times, couple of years ago, she'd received snide remarks concerning her budding breasts, once with an attempt made to pinch them; and a long time ago during Eid, she'd seen two girls around her age, ten, in charge of two small boys and a little girl, taking a ride on a rickety Ferris wheel, and every time the cradle with the five of them came creaking, rolling down, a couple of African boys waiting at the bottom would attempt to poke their fingers into the girls' panties—the older ones shrieked, the little girl looked terrified, all trapped in that cradle. The owner of the wheel was an Indian and simply grinned at the girls.

This time, though, as she started taking the round-about opposite the Odeon, she noticed four Indian boys sitting on the edge of the pavement, their feet on the road. They looked like the town's typical loafers—jostling each other shoulder to shoulder, sharing smokes, raucous. Respectable boys didn't sit outside like that, especially at this hour. Four men were playing whist on the roundabout, a small wick lamp burning near them. Behind the boys, next to the theatre, an African man sat roasting cassava and corn.

As she approached them the boys made a remark so obscene, later she couldn't even repeat it to herself; reciting "Ya Ali, Ya Ali," rapidly under her breath, she sped past them. A partly sucked orange came flying, hit her front wheel; she braked, too late realizing she shouldn't have. The bicycle stopped, keeled over, though Anaar saved herself in time from falling down. Her shame preserved, like Draupadi's in the legend.

She started telling off the boys: "Aren't you ashamed of yourselves—don't you have mothers and sisters of your own—" That always took care of grossness in men, the mention of their mothers and sisters. They laughed, made an obscene remark about sisters, but just then a white Cortina came by and stopped. She knew the driver, her friend Guli's mamu, Amir Uncle. He got out of the car and told off the boys, not too harshly but quite sternly; and he told off the men, who had been playing cards and not come to her aid. One of them spoke out impatiently, not even looking up from the game to waste his time, "What does she expect, wearing a skirt and riding a bicycle—and at this time!"

At which Amir Uncle said, "That's the school uniform, don't you know that—in which world do you live? Take a close look at the calendar next time and check the year!"

Another man said, "Keep her at home, she's of age."

The boys tee-heed. Nevertheless, one of them assisted Amir Uncle to lift the bicycle onto the roof rack, and Amir Uncle drove Anaar home, admonishing her all the way about how late it was for a girl. "Who is the drama teacher, anyway—Mr. Gregory? Mr. Fernandes?"

"Both," she told him.

Anaar was sixteen years old.

~

She was always a rebel, Anaar says, these many years later in Toronto. She and her husband of twenty-three years have agreed to a divorce, and I have just listed their house for sale. I have also agreed to help her find a place to stay, which goes beyond my duties as real estate agent. But I am also a mukhi, a sort of father in our community, though she is no more than two years younger than me. As we sit together in a coffee shop, after having looked at an apartment, I feel somewhat compromised. People do talk, though in this section of town hardly anybody would know us.

Always a rebel, she says—wanting to do different, waiting to get away—which is why, though only partly why, she decided to move to Canada.

"That bike, for instance—it was a ladies' bike even though it was bought for the use of both my brother and me—more for him since he was a boy."

They were mongoose and snake, she and her brother; hated each other to obsession. He was a year and a half younger and into bad company from the beginning.

The beginning was when her father died and her mother remarried. Her parents had lived upcountry in the town of Dodoma in central Tanzania. Her mother went to live with her new husband in Uganda, and later in Congo. The kids were parcelled off first separately to two relatives on her mother's side, and shortly thereafter reunited in the home of their father's younger brother. They were treated well, perhaps too well. Anaar was nine. Their aunt and uncle had a son, their only child, a year after Anaar and her brother were adopted.

Anaar never forgot her parents' home, Dodoma, the gulley—or alley—in which they lived, the tinsmiths knocking pots and pans into shape, the sweetmeat shop, the open drain, the quarrels among the women, the local crazy shuffling along followed by a train of boys. She spoke about that home to hurt her uncle and aunt when she wanted to taunt them, when she needed something so badly she didn't care about anybody else: she was an orphan, sort of, was her defence of last resort.

But she helped to raise their child, Azim, who always called her his sister; and she cooked in the house, especially when both her aunt and uncle were needed in the shop during month-end rush.

*

By my teenage years I lived with my family in Upanga, an Indian suburb closer to the schools and the beach, away from the bustle of Kariakoo and Uhuru Street where Indian shops serviced African needs. I think I saw Anaar for the first time after school one Saturday (which was a half day) when I came walking along her street accompanying a friend to his home. She came gliding up on the opposite side of the street, erect on her bike seat, quite modest in her green box-pleat skirt and white blouse—the school uniform—her hair done up in a long pigtail. I remember stopping and turning around to watch as she went by. She alighted swiftly outside a corner store, stood the bike, which a boy, her brother, then took and pedalled away. He went past us, taking his hands off the handlebars, stretching them out sideways in an act of bravado.

That vision of a slim, fair, thin-faced girl approaching on her bicycle is, in the constellation of memories of my hometown, a bright star, something that draws a wistful smile. We looked down our noses at Kariakoo, those of us from Upanga. Contrasted with Kariakoo's dusty hustle and bustle, its homes huddled behind shopfronts or stacked closely above the stores in apartments, we had what we would now call townhouses, with ample gardens, and friendly alleys and playing fields. But Kariakoo from that day onward also had this genie, the only girl I had seen in Dar on a bicycle; the place was now home to a certain mystery, an enigma.

She had, as I recall further from that day, a certain sternness in demeanour, an intensity in the eyes as she concentrated on the road in front of her; and the tight pigtail gave a prominence to her cheekbones and forehead.

She is not as thin-faced now, but it is hard not to super-pose that face from long ago upon the one before me and see a match. And it is as hard not to feel the force of an enigma, even now. Her voice is soft and I've not seen her laugh, but she smiles warmly and searchingly as she looks into your eyes.

~

Her Amir Uncle, Anaar's girlfriend Guli would say, was more like a brother or cousin; he was a bachelor and liked to play games—"You should see him at the picnics"—and flirted with the women. He was not as old as the other uncles either.

Anaar too began to call him Amir Uncle. And to her too he was more like an elder brother who said silly things sometimes and made jokes and was protective. As a person from Upanga, who worked as a comptroller at the European firm of Twentsche Overseas Motors, he had a status; at work he wore white shorts, shirt, and stockings, with black shoes, as the Europeans did. Before, she had hardly been aware of him, but now that she knew him, he seemed to be everywhere, known to everyone. One Sunday she went with Guli to their family picnic and she saw for herself what her friend had meant. Amir Uncle was the star of the event—he played cricket with the boys, using a coconut branch for bat and a tennis ball; afterwards with the younger men and women he played hutu-tutu, the territorial game with two teams, and he entertained everybody by his teasing and baiting of the opponents. He helped in making tea, and after tea he played cards.

His only handicap, if you could call it that, was that he was not very tall.

"Why doesn't Amir Uncle marry?" Anaar asked Guli. "He could get a wife like that—" she snapped her fingers smartly.

"He's too picky," Guli replied. "All those single girls who were at the picnic are simply dying to see whom he'll pick. One of these days. . . ."

The "single girls" were more like women, ten years older than either of them, and none of them looked very pretty to Anaar.

~

"None of them married properly," Anaar says to me. "It's amazing isn't it, they were in their twenties and their lives had run out."

There were five of these women and, as we observe together, all had completed high school, which was a rare feat in their time. One never married, four married widowers with children. Two died of breast cancer, one was murdered in Miami; one is divorced and lives somewhere in Toronto. We discuss her whereabouts, Anaar and I. In Toronto you locate a person not by the area they live in— this is a large city, spread out—but by the mosque they attend; that's like a postal code—and if you think about it, guarantees where you'll find the person on a Friday evening. I am the mukhi of Don Mills; Anaar has been attending York Mills; and this woman we spoke of goes to Eglinton. A far cry, this geometry, from the one in our memories.

~

Amir Uncle brought movie passes for Guli and Anaar, and since the two girls had to be accompanied, he went with them. They liked Indian movies, which he didn't much care for, and this made them giggle to themselves since it was *they* who were younger and supposed to be more modern. She didn't mind that he made fun of the movies afterwards—you went for the songs and the romance and (as everyone who loved them knew) you simply ignored their lack of realism—the last-minute recognition of a lost son, the weepy hospital scene, or the obviously artificial full moon behind a tree! After every such outing with Amir Uncle, Anaar would be bursting with praises for him, until her aunt finally began calling him "your Amir Uncle."

With Amir Uncle, too, she got a taste of things they could not quite afford in her family—such as ice cream at Naaz Restaurant in the evenings, and the drive on Ocean Road to look at all the beautiful houses of the Europeans and other rich people and stop later by the sea and listen in silence to the waves. A taste of that other life, of well-being, which she so longed for. Where she lived, by seven the street was dark and quiet—the shops would be all closed, their owners huddled upstairs or behind the stores with their families and radios. There would be news on the radio, perhaps followed by a drama, and two nights a week half an hour of pop music, Monday's "Happy Returns" and Friday's "Favourites." Lights out at ten, the absolute latest.

Amir Uncle came like a ray of light, a happy beam, into that drab life.

~

"If there's one thing I don't miss from those days, it's those still, still nights," she says. "And yet there was a strange mystery to them . . . something unforgettable . . . we were more religious then, too."

"Yes."

"Are you religious?"

I cast an appropriate stare at her. "I am a mukhi," I answer, as if that explains everything.

The coffee shop on North Toronto's Yonge Street is abustle with wealthy young couples out shopping. Time was, on this drag you'd find maybe one or two eating places open this late and serving "Canadian coffee" (Maxwell House institutional brand); now the coffee houses selling fresh and fancy brews sit cheek to jowl, and you can bet in the course of time, perhaps in the lull after Christmas, a few of them will be smothered right out of the competition, what with an American chain joining in the fray and upping the ante.

We've come here having inspected a show unit for a condo development coming up in the area, one of those with fancy names like Governor's Terrace to make you feel you are partaking in the opulence previously reserved for colonial British sahibs. She liked it and thinks she'll rent an apartment in the area while she waits for possession.

"You're selling her house—you're not obliged to find her a place to stay," my wife Farida chides.

"It's good business," I respond. "Besides, she's a woman alone and—"

"Exactly."

"Don't tell me you're jealous—"

She smiles.

"I am the mukhi," I continue, "and it's our duty to help—don't forget, you're mukhiani-*maa*—"

Maa means "mother," but in a respectful way, though these days it's not always likely to be taken as a compliment even by grandmas.

"We were in school together, I am hardly her mother," Farida says, though the term does please her, I'm surprised.

Farida looks no older than Anaar at all.

"Did you find out why," she says, raising an eye, "you know—she did what she did at the funeral?"

"No—I don't think she knows that I know."

"Not a good detective, are we?"

~

She had been seeing Amir Uncle for more than a year before she realized she'd been doing exactly that. There would be times when Guli failed to show up at a planned outing and Anaar would be with him by herself—except for her cousin Azim, who always came with her; that was nothing unusual, girls took along a little brother the same way they would a shawl or a sweater. And Azim was so quiet, it was almost as if he were not there.

When school holidays came around, Guli and Anaar decided they would attend early morning mosque, which began at four every day. Amir Uncle would give them a ride. But after the first two mornings, Guli couldn't get up, felt too lazy, and so it was Anaar and Amir Uncle, of course with Azim, who went. On the way back Amir Uncle would take the two of them for a drive past the seashore; one day he said to Anaar, "Why don't I teach you how to drive?"

It was the most thrilling thought for Anaar; to be able to drive a car! So she and Amir Uncle, with the quiet, half-absent Azim in the back of the car, went for driving lessons early in the morning after mosque. And after the holidays, it was the same trio who went to a movie, the Little Theatre, or somewhere else. Her guardians believed she went out with her friend Guli, and she didn't tell them otherwise. Neither did her silent chaperone Azim. Anaar believed that he too liked the outings in the car, and the treats, and Amir Uncle. Sometimes she would receive a message through Guli, about a play or a dance performance, the office Christmas party, or even a tennis or cricket match. Twice there were presents, purportedly from her friend Guli—a bead necklace and a gold bangle—and her aunt and uncle despaired of how to repay the gifts.

But one day Mrs. Daya, the gossip across the street, alerted her aunt, who interrogated Azim, and the fat was in the fire.

In the next several weeks Anaar declined all invitations from Amir Uncle, which were brought of course by their messenger Guli: to attend the final of the Youth Drama Competition, for which tickets were so scarce; to attend the New Year's party at Twentsche Overseas Motors; to go and hear a qawali recital by the famed Shakila Banu Bhopali and her troupe from India. Finally, one time Amir Uncle followed her in his car as she was returning from school on her bicycle; she stopped, at the Odeon; her bike went on the roof rack and she sat in the car. And she told him, "It's not right—to go out with a man—you took advantage of me."

He was aghast, his face contorted in pain—"But I am in love with you," he said. "I want to marry you! I want to take you into my arms and show you the world, I want to send you to a college—even to Dar University! What future do you have where you are? You want to get married one day, don't you? Do you want to run a shop all your life? Don't you think I'm a good man, with faith in God, and honourable, with good prospects in a foreign firm? Let me give you the world—if you didn't care for me would you have come with me before? Have I been without honour so far—"

"Why didn't you tell me your intentions before?" she asked tearfully, but they were reconciled. He dropped her outside the store, brought down her bicycle from the roof with the help of a servant, greeted her aunt and uncle with "God bless," and drove away.

They glared at Anaar: "Didn't we tell you—"

"Amir Uncle and I care for each other and we want to get married," she declared, and blushed. What she said was not only radical and insubordinate; calling her suitor "Uncle" made her look ridiculous and childish, hardly to be taken seriously.

"Don't be silly," her aunt said. "The man is old enough to be your father!"

"He's not!"

But he was.

"I went to school with him," her uncle said quietly to Anaar, "and he was two classes ahead of me."

Suddenly she was at the centre of a storm: neighbours, aunts, even girlfriends began talking to her of the future; how young and beautiful she was, she could have her pick of husbands. Two proposals of marriage were brought to her, both decent, from men in their mid-twenties. Her guardians promised to send her to college when she finished school; they proposed a holiday in Uganda for the coming break. And an elderly aunt put it to her bluntly: "When you are forty he will be an elderly bapa of sixty, will he be able to satisfy you?" Did this old aunt mean what Anaar thought she meant? Anaar's knowledge of what men and women did to produce children was scant; she knew men had erections, and girls called penises "sticks," and recently when some relations from upcountry had come to visit and she had to share her bed with her ten-year-old cousin Azim, she found it, for the first time, rather awkward. She couldn't quite tell why. She felt she'd been touched.

What thrilled her, however, was a sense of importance. She was being courted by everyone. It would be *her* decision what she did, that she knew. A sense of independence and maturity, of responsibility, came over her. Power. Amir Uncle, who had been like a prince descended from the sky, begged her, "Please don't call me 'Uncle,'" but that was so difficult! And he pleaded, "I'm only fifteen years older, not twenty, as they say." He could bring witnesses, name references, he would bring a copy of his birth certificate, which he had applied for. And best of all, there were reports that he had turned intensely devout, spending long times at the takht in mosque, beseeching the Lord—asking Him for *her*, Anaar Dhalla!

When the formal proposal for marriage came from his family, Anaar was two months past her eighteenth birthday. It was brought by Amir's (she *had* to call him that now) mother, a tall stout woman who ran a nursery school, who came with two of his sisters (one a teacher, the other a steno) and three elders from the community. The visitors were seated, tea was produced, with biscuits. Anaar hovered at the door to the sitting room (which was also her aunt and uncle's bedroom) and one of the elders began:

"You know why we are here—the matter's already at an advanced stage, so let's not tarry." The boy's qualities were listed; the girl was of age; and most of all, it seemed the couple was intent on the union. "Nowhere in our tradition is it mentioned that age be a barrier to a willing couple's marriage."

The aunt and uncle said they had to consult the girl, and of course the rest of the family. They felt they had been misled by the boy, who had come into the girl's life as an uncle.

Humorous comments were made about the boldness of love—not to say its folly. And after all, hadn't everyone heard of uncles and aunts younger than their nieces and nephews? The boy came highly recommended, was truly a gem; all three elders personally vouched for him.

As parting shot, one of the sisters, the steno, remarked, "After all, the girl is your trust and you should do what's in her interest, even though it may get difficult for you around the house once she's gone."

It was a mild taunt. The guardians said they would consider the proposal, as was natural, and the visitors left in good spirits. All three women insisted on giving Anaar a kiss.

By this time any doubts Anaar had (and there had been queasy moments) had vanished; she wanted to get married, to get away to Upanga, a life in the suburbs, a car, her own room and house, all the things she couldn't have now. When her aunt and uncle tried to prevail upon her, she told them cruelly what Amir's sister had only hinted at: "If I were your own daughter, you wouldn't let me miss this golden opportunity to move up in life. You only need me here to help you around the house and shop."

The engagement was duly announced. But once this hurdle was past, the consent of marriage given, there was no acrimony left over, the two families were like one big family. And Amir was a most attentive and charming fiancé who bore no grudges.

~

"We'll hardly see her now," Farida says, watching me pour our tea.

It's Friday evening, mosque time, and we usually dispense with dinner on this day, making do with a tea and something light later in the evening.

"I said we'll hardly see her now," she says.

What I say, in agreement, is a straight-faced lie. I'm not even surprised how easily it comes, though I'm not a habitual liar. Yes, there's a feeling akin to a weight on the heart, but not enough to crush; there's no real dread or terror at the possibilities I may be invoking. That ability to feel finely has been lost—what with thoughts of mortality and anxieties about the children, one is too far from the precipice, there's nothing fragile left to break, all is custom, routine; affection and habit. That's not necessarily so bad.

Anaar has now a place of her own, and her house has found a buyer, too. She has no longer need of my services as an agent. But she continues to draw me, to her apartment on Yonge or the coffee shop down below, to which I occasionally head like an automaton oblivious to anything but the moment before me.

"Did she act strangely with you at all?" my wife asks. "Did you find out what's wrong with her? Why would she spit on a corpse—when we've all come to mourn and forgive, at a holy place, with so many people around? She's not gone crazy, has she?"

"Perhaps she couldn't forgive him."

"What can't one forgive in death? What can be so grievous?"

"Beats me."

At another time, in the past, I would have told her without a thought; this time I feel beholden to a confidence. Why keep this secret from her, develop a niche in my heart for another soul? I am at a loss to explain. In the past few weeks I've quite lost my head, though if you saw me you wouldn't notice, I'd be your same old jolly caring mukhi with a patient ear and ready smile, with a large friendly network that supplies me prospective clients and business tips out of gratitude. Deep within me I've become victim to memories and images from the past, perilous yearnings; and an uncontrollable, you might say suicidal, desire to put it all down.

In Dar we had two kinds of pretty girls: the tall and thin kind, with long hair, traditional—Anaar's type; and the shorter ones with softer features and modish short hair—Farida's type. Of course, nowadays all of them have short hair.

Farida was from an established though unaffected family who owned one of the city's two bakeries and were known for their services to the community. Her manner reflected this background; she was not shy, nor haughtily aloof, but her easy, friendly nature seemed curbed by a wary reserve that demanded its proper distance. If you were thick-skinned, as teenage boys tended to be, she was adept with an appropriate and quite arrogant snub, as I once found out. We used to return from our separate schools in separate groups, boys and girls, and one day I let fly out a silly jibe in her direction, pertaining to her family's business, in the belief that to tease was a way to win a girl's heart. I went home red-faced. Then some months later to my immense excitement I saw her alone, straggling behind her group; I was alone too and hurried to join her. She was friendly, her twinkling eyes recalling that snub, which had already earned me a lasting nickname among the boys. And so we began our small incidental meetings, and without any formality fell in with each other as boyfriend and girlfriend. A childhood romance. A girl to be close to; a boy to tell things to.

"The wedding night," Anaar says with a tinge of a blush.

From my vantage point up here in her living room, Yonge Street stretches down, in a series of yellow street-lamps and moving car lights, all the way south to the lakeshore, to the blinking CN Tower. It is beautiful, the street, the city, at night, a magical scape of thousands of lights. And up here, except for our voices, all is quiet, hushed. From what she says, I form my own picture of what transpired that night that traumatized her so.

The hotel picked for the night by Amir and his family, perhaps by accident as they claimed, but most likely because of an offered discount, was well located by the sea, but that Saturday it clamoured with the din of dancing and music from the lounge directly below the couple's room. She lost her mood, which was not helped by the groom's family and friends coming to inspect the room, make sly remarks, and have photographs taken—all part of a repulsive and new tradition then, mercifully no longer in existence now. Amir apologized—he was always nice—and promised that the rooms for their honeymoon, at the national parks, would all be perfect.

Amir was somewhat limp, I surmise, nervous; inexperienced, she says, though I am not sure what she means, experience being evidence of moral depravity in those days. She herself had an inkling of what was expected—from books (she refuses to name any, with a coy smile) and talking to a girl whose sister had recently married. She was a healthy girl, she says. At some point in their tentative foreplay she mounted him and took her pleasure. At the critical moment for her, her eyes fell upon the wall in front of her, saw a small bright spot some three fourths of the way up. The room was in partial darkness, a dim pervasive glow intruding into their privacy from the square courtyard outside, with its garden of rocks and plants and large globe lights under which couples courted. It was, Anaar says, of that spot on the wall, a blink of light that quickly disappeared, leaving behind a speck to blend in with the other shadows in the room. Momentarily she feared that she and her husband had been spied upon through an aperture in the wall. Such incidents had been heard of. But she convinced herself the world was not really so evil, that the spot was due to some incidental reflection from outside, and went to sleep more anxious about her future.

The next morning, though, getting out of bed while he was in the shower, she inspected the wall above the headboard and discovered a round hole the width of her little finger. She didn't tell her husband. All she wanted was to get out of there as quickly as possible, though she couldn't very well deny her husband and their friends the brunch at the hotel that was part of the wedding celebration.

That incident, that night, ruined for her the rest of her life; her interest in her husband, in having children (though she did have a son). It filled her with depression, dread, hatred. If she didn't take her life, it was due to that hate, for one man.

"Who was he?"

"As we checked out of the hotel, at the front desk sat the owner's son—Salim Damani. He grinned at us and said something I dare not repeat—but it's been playing in my head over and over like a tape ever since. It was he who had been peeping at us. In that moment he had stolen my entire existence, robbed me of my faith, any belief in anything . . . and he knew that I knew."

She looks at me with those intense eyes in that fine

face. I realize again how soft her voice is, not having risen even once, and yet strangely so full of expression.

"He had intruded into and defiled my most private, my woman's moment. I could have killed him, gouged his eyes out—whenever I saw him standing outside the mosque in the evening with the other men; I could have torn out the flesh from that pocked face. One day on Jamhuri Street I saw his wife and small child crossing the road—he married not long after me—I was driving our Cortina, and there they were and I was glaring at them in all madness—but some good angel held me back. Salim was inside a shop and he came tearing out, perhaps having seen me through the door or shop window. I don't know what I might have done in those days. Outwardly I was normal, I had a husband and a son, but inside I was seething, a wounded female seeking desperately somehow to avenge that offence, that violence done to me. How many times I wished he would simply die and rid me of him. Whenever I passed the mosque and read the chalkboard containing the latest death announcement, I would wish it were him, that if I rubbed out the name written there and wrote his instead, he would truly die.

"When it became possible to come to Canada, Amir and I were among the first to apply—I couldn't have stayed there a day longer than necessary, where *he* resided, that piece of filth who continued to pollute me with every sight I had of him.

"I imagined him festering in Dar, in the heat and mud and the growing potholes and the smells of garbage not picked up. . . ."

While she removed herself to an antithetical cooler universe of temperance and restraint, order and form, sliding noiselessly into the future.

In Toronto, Dar's Asians found themselves in the new high-rises of Don Mills, which reminded one more and more of the hometown neighbourhoods as new immigrants, old acquaintances, arrived. You left on the 100 or the 26 bus to go to, to search for, work; weekends you shopped till you dropped, from discount store to discount store, across the city, when a dollar meant so much more. Remembered from this distance in time, they were days of shame, when none of us had cars and we travelled in flocks on public transit fearing racial taunts and attacks. Anaar found a job almost immediately, like many of the women, as a typist; Amir languished from one unsuitable job to the next. He was in his forties, not especially suited to anything though capable and more than willing, and was soon humiliated and broken, all his former stature gone. But they worked hard, put up the down payment for a car, then for a house in a new development.

A rented room in the basement of the Flemingdon Park Mall was the first mosque. There, every evening, especially Fridays, you went to be part of one big communal family. You exchanged news from home (the worse it got there, the better you felt here) and met new arrivals, you found out about all the specials at the food, clothing, and furniture stores in town. One Friday evening, her eye alighting upon a new attendee at this makeshift mosque, her heart sank and she gave a whimper: "Y'Allah!" It was Salim Damani—older, humbler:

taking around a brazier smoking with incense among the male congregation. It did not take her long to detect Salim's wife sitting two rows in front of her.

It was as well she and her husband moved to their house in York Mills. But after a year, like many others, the Damanis followed suit and she kept running into him at the new mosque there. Of course he was now a respectable member of the community. But she continued to hate him with the bitterest bile, never replied to his unctuously uttered "God bless, sister."

Once, in front of people, he manipulated her into shaking hands with him, and on another occasion, during a community picnic, when everyone had joined in for a game of "dodge-the-ball," he put himself in a position close behind her. She gave a howl of anguish, which in the merriment of the occasion no one else quite heeded; but he knew. And she was sure he had done it on purpose.

She retired from the game, went home early. And that night she cried her heart out, wept and wept, no one could stop her, until she'd washed herself out, and fell asleep.

Years passed. Her son grew up. She and her husband held office in the community, earned respect, became established. The fire in her abated, but did not die altogether. Finally, twenty years after their arrival in Toronto, her husband brought home the news one morning from the mosque—

"Salim Damani died—last night."

She gasped. "How?"

"Heart attack—while working around the house. His wife says he was tired and had sat down to rest in the living room in front of the TV—that's where he passed away. Did you know he was part owner of two hotels?"

"Do you think I overdid it—my anger?" she asks.

I look away, at the ceiling, which is dark and in shadow, at the glory of lights that is Yonge Street down below. How can I ever imagine what it meant to her, that one scorching moment in the life of a tender, raw nineteen-year-old girl back home, and what that moment did to all the other moments of her life? But I feel a heavy sense of sadness in me, I cannot tell you quite why. And I also feel a hint of anger, or bitterness, I know not where to direct it.

The Sky to Stop Us

His wife had left him. Her sports car was not in the driveway, the pool area normally cacophonous at this hour with the screams and laughter of his daughter Zafira and her neighbourhood friends seemed weirdly forlorn; there was no sign of the kitchen having seen use recently, and there were four phone messages, the first one from 12:12, as one of their friends precisely logged it. And there was this note on the table in the family room: *I've gone away for a while with Z, will call you later. I want to think things over for myself.—A.*

How serious was it? He brought his chilled beer glass to his chin and mulled over that, feeling suddenly uncontrollably tearful. It's the tiredness; you want to come home at night to pour out your frustrations and be comforted, not for this. What did it mean? Had it been coming? Had he seen the symptoms? She had taken to making certain kinds of statements lately, to chaff him— so he had interpreted them. *One of these days I should leave you.* The idea had seemed unthinkable. The remarks would needle him, for how easily they came to her; why make them, he had thought, why the empty threats? Not so empty now. And right in the midst of a major deal worth millions, many millions perhaps . . . right when the world was his, theirs, for those with the guts and the smarts to take and hold in their hands; opportunities, vistas, were opening up before them one after another without end. Why would she want to put brakes on that, deny him all that?

The telephone rang, quickly he picked it up. It was his father. Nazir's fingers tightened around the receiver; just what he needed at this moment, like a hole in the head, to comfort his lonely old father in his cluttered room at the Victoria Park senior citizens' apartments. Did you take your walk, he asked dutifully, calmly, you need the exercise—Yes, said the old man, grateful for the attention, he had walked the length of the corridor three times; Are you going to mosque today, you should, to get out—the bus steps were too high for his arthritic knees, came the reply, he could go if had a car ride; Take a taxi,

then, haven't I told you you can? And so on. Following
which, critiques of various people. The cleaning woman
Zarin had stolen his slippers and he had asked her not to
return. Why would Zarin steal your old slippers? How
should *I* know? It was no use arguing with him. Let him
ramble on about the woman across the hall, the Pakistani
man two floors above, the other woman who was only
pretending to be a senior for the cheap rent although she
had the strength of a horse. . . . And after that, a list of
things required from the shops—soap, paper flowers,
paper plates. . . . Nazir imagined himself physically
exploding while listening to all this, his blood gushing
out of his heart and ears, his guts spewing all over the
place, and his father's crackling voice going on and on
and on like the rusty springs of a rickety truck on an endless road. . . . Give the man a chance, he's lonely.

By the time his dad hung up, there was a message
waiting, from his own son in Montreal. He called back,
found Shaf.

Hi, Dad. Mum told me—

Where is she?

I can't tell you that—

Why not? Don't you care about me—about us? About
the family unit—

Take it easy, Dad. I promised. I can't tell. Not now.
Give her a chance, let's work it out.

You tell me where she is and I'll work it out with her,
I promise you.

Like he'd done all these years. Given her everything
she wanted, and more. A million-dollar house that all
their friends drooled over; a sports car of her own; a

housemaid; the kids in private schools; dinners ordered in or eaten out; parties, cruises, holidays. They had gone from rags to riches in two decades, together, why would she do this to him? All he asked for was the time to do what he had to do. And that had been her constant quibble: you're not home long enough, like other husbands and fathers. Do they have what we have? he would ask hotly. Of course not.

No mean achievement that, rags to riches. They had done the immigrants' apartment route in Don Mills, gone hustling after cheap prices from one end of town to another, considered themselves fortunate to be consuming fast foods and calories as a treat . . . all that, yet at work they hit the glass ceiling early on, she in a lawyer's office where a British accent and white skin meant you were visible and up front, while she was relegated to the dungeons of the archives, too reserved, too nervous to ask for more, for her right to opportunity; and he as a loan clerk in a bank downtown where the manager craved nothing more than to push him out, which he eventually did. But he, Nazir, a grocer's son, did two things right: he bought a rental unit on Spadina when property there was dirt cheap, in partnership with three others, a Bengali and two Chinese, and just before real estate prices went boom in the eighties; and while at the bank he was smart enough to invest in the money market, watching how others made their fortunes. Then one day he told Almas, Love, you don't have to work for those sons of bitches, you stay home and bring up little Shaf here and that girl who's on the way. Where we're going there's only the sky to stop us, and if you recall your high school science, even the sky's an illusion. And he himself told his manager to piss off, to put it mildly. He sold off his portfolio for a huge profit; with his partners he renovated the property on Spadina, converted it into an international hostel, sold it. He was rolling. He bought a bigger hotel on the Don Valley that was badly managed and made it turn a profit; then sold it. He was growing; his partners were growing; Toronto was growing. And now to *spurn* that, for some sentimental reason, because he didn't have time to play baseball with the kids ... or sit with them for dinner, because he was out there making sure his son had a Honda Civic to take to college and his fees would be paid at Harvard if he made it ... which he didn't, but McGill wasn't so bad either.

After a couple of whiskies with crackers and cheese and a previous day's meat samosas, he watched *Star Trek* on TV. It was one of the few things he shared with his son Shaf. What he liked about the Trekkie stories were the limitless vistas in them, the endless universe, so to speak; anything was possible; there were no traditions to hold you back, no boundaries. Of course, the details in these stories were most likely all wrong or too trivial; but it was the attitude that counted. There's no limit. Think big; think smart; think new.

He had felt hurt, initially, at his wife's desertion; he now was angry. How *dare* anyone try to rein in another against their very nature; try to cage a lion. He had been to a zoo once in his life and hated it. To see lions in cages! When he'd seen them stalking, chasing a herd of zebra on the Serengeti, jumping on the poor helpless one at the back, caught unawares!

The TV was on mute, the house was deathly quiet; the phone refused to ring. Tears fell freely down his cheeks. However much he valued his freedom, he knew that he needed his family, the stable base it provided, from which he could head off in whatever direction he wished. His victories meant nothing without being able to share it with them. That's why he had given Almas everything he could, toned down his wild habits, turned away from women he could have had on the side, and become a pussycat at home. He loved his family, his children. His wife? In a way, yes.

Because I knew her love for me was not really of the passionate kind, any more than mine was for her, there were some regrets there, on both sides. I always felt that and so I had to have my own personal passion. She was a Nairobi girl thrown together with us Dar guys and girls in the early seventies in Toronto when we lived at Lawrence and Don Mills; everyone was getting paired off and there seemed not much choice. We liked each other; and she was smarting from a love back home of which I have only been able to guess so far. We married, but I could always sense her admiration for the easygoing types, the professors and intellectuals who liked to gab; but I was a grocer's son, and I'm going to conquer the world, I told her cockily. Why don't you simply enjoy life, she would say. Easy to say that, but she always liked luxury, the nanny and big houses and flashy cars.

The next day he woke up to a cold bed beside him; he choked at the prospect that this would be a permanent state of affairs. He washed, dressed, and went for coffee at a nearby café. He wished to brood over the situation, plan a course of action to woo her back. It would not be easy, but it could be done. Meanwhile there was today's meeting, claiming urgent attention. A group from out west was in town with a prospect for his group of hoteliers. They were medical people, doctors with flourishing careers, money pouring in, and the itch to invest big time. The proposal was ambitious: to open a full-facility medical hotel for the wealthy and those privately covered. Insurance companies from Hartford were in town and willing to listen. The Ramada chain was sniffing around the edges. This looked big, if it worked out, with global potential.

The guy who had approached him with the idea was currently from Nanaimo, BC, originally from Dar and a year younger than Nazir. And this is just what he couldn't stress enough to Almas: the money's for the grabbing out there, people with half the balls are raking it in; do you want me to sit on my butt watching the sun set and feeling my life ebb away with every breath?

Walji—he was the guy who had brought him the multimillion-dollar scheme; his folks used to own a small goods store a couple of blocks away back in Dar. As grocers, Nazir's parents were marginally better off than Walji's; Nazir recalled a short, frail-looking boy walking to and from school with his brother and sister. The snivelling sort, no guts. Nazir would tease the three siblings sometimes, occasionally throw stones at them, on the way home, for he was the rough type. Now here was the same Walji running a doctors' syndicate, just as he Nazir ran a hoteliers' and property managers', and they shook hands and let's take it away from here. What a world. What a country. What d'you mean I think only of making money?

I am building this country for you and me, I'm paving the road with velvet for you kids to walk on with ease.

That was the problem, wasn't it; these kids had everything they needed, everything taken care of, all they lacked was ambition and drive. What a disappointment. Same thing for her. So much at hand, time to fritter away, to learn new things, and all she worries about are the kids, and what other people think, and then she feels lonely with nothing to do. Here, he said once, take this round sum of money, play the stock market, make money, or lose it, make life interesting. She bought some stocks; techs were high. But then every initiative, every decision regarding the portfolio—buy this, wait a while longer for that, buy Dell, dump Eli Lilly—had to be his.

Hi, Shaf . . . calling his son over the mobile. Hi, Dad. You going to tell me where she is hiding herself? Remember you saying once that what you hated most was your mum and dad fighting? I can't, Dad. I promised. Jesus, where are your priorities? Please, Dad. All right— are you coming home to visit? Maybe.

Maybe. What did that mean? Were the three of them partners in a conspiracy now—against this big bad guy who thinks only of money and can't spare a moment for them? God, the distraction of family life . . . and yet you couldn't do without it, that part of existence needed to be taken care of . . . like sex. Yes, that too. It seemed he had rediscovered his vigour in recent months, was reliving his pubescence; as if the body had realized time was short and in desperation was cashing in the reserves. And now she's gone, what to do.

That morning at the business meeting they came

upon a possible stumbling block: a floor or two of an upscale hotel turned into a medical unit, would that keep regular customers away? Who wants to be close to the sick and possibly dying, even if they're rich? The sites for such units would be crucial. Perhaps have entire hotels dedicated to medical care? More research was needed; meanwhile, the utmost secrecy—from competitors, and from media and the NDP types who hadn't realized the days of socialized medicine were over. And perhaps Intercontinental or Hilton or the Oberois would have to be brought in for their access to quality clients. Lunch was too heavy, after which a tour of the hotels, then an informal exchange of ideas. A full day, exhausting, just the way he loved it. At night, alone, nobody waiting up for him, except his bottle of Scotch. And *Star Trek* and the outer edges of an expanding universe.

He dreamt. What's more, he remembered it when he woke up in the middle of the night, heart thumping, in a cold sweat. God God God. . . . They were on safari in Africa, they were standing with other people in a field of sorts, he saw Zafira running out of the crowd and in front of a pride of lions under a tree, while the others watched fascinated, and only he, he Nazir, could sense the imminent danger, knew the lions were hungry, and he shouted at her frantically, then dashed after her to pick her up just as a lioness came bounding up to take her away. . . .

He couldn't sleep after that. Would half his bed be vacant always, right through old age; would this lovely house be empty; was it a condominium for him after all . . . or another woman, but he didn't want to start over again, with another shape, another face and smell beside him. . . . He was too much a creature of habit, especially now. Perhaps there could yet be someone somewhere who would really love him with a passion, perhaps he should give himself that chance . . . though did he have time for love?

He recalled a reunion among friends, his old pal Haji visiting from the States; Haji the handsome, free, and easygoing academic; and she once calling Haji by her husband's name, Nazir; and his ears pricked up, and he hurt a little, but only for a moment, there was so much on his mind, and what could you do about such a situation, such a buried feeling anyway. Only he wished she could see what was obvious to everybody else there, how envious Handsome Haji was of what Nazir had made of his life, how hungry these professors were for just a little more money, and at the end of the day what did they have to show for themselves? No Einsteins among them, that was certain.

The first thing next morning, a call from his father. Yes, yes, Dad, I'll do your shopping, can't you give me even a day, but he knew all his dad wanted was to speak to him . . . and the more his dad called for no reason at all, which meant just to be able to speak to somebody, the more impatient Nazir got with him.

And so, coffee and croissant at his neighbourhood café; a tour of his properties. On Elm Street at Crescent International Hostel, the Portuguese manager was obviously skimming off some, letting rooms without recording them; which was expected, but there was an Albanian he had earmarked for the job, a former engineer no less, who looked trustworthy. Meanwhile the Portuguese had to be watched. Perhaps a job at the hotel on Don Valley, a promotion of sorts, and as soon as he showed his true colours, as he was certain to do, push him off.

Bad business at the hostel on Danforth. They were converting it into upscale, in an area fast growing fashionable and touristy; which meant the former occupants had to be squeezed out with higher rates and room renovations to go with them. There were three units left to be converted, their occupants a single Indian woman, another woman who was a single mother of two, and a retired Bangladeshi couple. That's what the manager reminded him of over the mobile. When he arrived at the manager's office, the tenants were sitting outside to appeal the notice of rate hike. They didn't have a legal option to speak of, Nazir knew. The single mother was a white woman of thirty or so, and the Indian woman—he glared at her, avoided her eyes, looked away.

But she latched on to him. Mr. Nazir, I know you; in Gujarati. Help me please, we are as one— It's not in my hands, he told her, throwing glances at the other tenants; then tautly in English: Pay the new rate and you can stay. But how can I, Mr. Nazir. . . .

He felt dirty, he shouldn't have come. Hadn't he resolved he was beyond this low-level supervision? But for a business to run successfully you have to be in touch at all levels. Dirt was part of the risk, the cost of business.

That look from her, so piteous. How can you do that, Nazir? But this is the business I entered into; it has to be done right. Someone else in my shoes would do the same, or worse. Give them a month's notice of the new rates, he told the manager. If they can't pay they must vacate.

On his way to his car, he paused at a neighbouring building that had begun to interest him recently, a dilapidated structure, but for that very reason full of potential. Preoccupied by its possibilities, he drove off to shop for his father.

Paper flowers; aloe extract; Froot Loops—"good for my digestion"—pure bull; peanut butter, for rubbing into his arthritic knees; paraffin for laxative; vacuum cleaner bags; deboned chicken, which he normally wouldn't buy, but his son was paying; tortilla wraps to use as rotis.

The apartment was hideous, reflecting his mother's aesthetic sense when she was alive. Oversized and excessive furniture mostly with artificial veneer, assorted gewgaws to add decor, from plastic flowers to statuettes; the TV was on purely for its noise value. A heady mix of odours always in attendance: milk and perfumed bathroom cleaners.

Nazir put the shopping bags on the dining table, looked around, said, If you're not watching the TV why don't you turn it off, which his father dutifully did, saying, Sit and I'll bring tea. To which Nazir said, still standing, Do you need anything else? Yes, but sit for a while, won't you—you must be busy, I guess. . . . Yes, I have still a few things to do. You youngsters do too much, no rest, no time to sit down and chat, always busy. . . . Well—I'll give you a call later, Nazir told him; then after the briefest pause for a response, he left, feeling guilty as hell.

There was simply nothing to talk about. When they met, they didn't shake hands, didn't exchange hugs. No heart-to-heart between father and son, no opening of a couple of beers and talk of old times, learning family history before it was too late, no long walks together to discuss the kids and their future. He felt awkward before his father. He could not recall when he had last sat down with the old man, laughed with him over something. The truth was that he felt no love whatsoever for his father. That was the truth, naked and brutal. Why brutal?— because it wasn't right; he knew that. But he couldn't help it. Of course, this made it easier to forget the old man's existence between telephone calls. And no one else at home had any love for father-in-law and grand-dad either. Nazir had thought often about it, his coldness, his lack of tenderness toward his father, mulling over it usually in traffic, while returning from visiting Dad, or having just made his dutiful daily call on the mobile. Had he felt anything for his dad, ever?

Father sat in their grocery shop day in, day out, in striped pyjama pants and white singlet, except when relieved by Mother, when he had his lunch and took a nap afterwards. He liked to pick his crotch, luxuriously, in those pyjamas of his. The shop, and the mosque in the evening, kept him occupied, and the children—four boys and a girl, who was the youngest—did not spend much time in his presence. Once a month he gave them all their school fees, with some ceremony, until they were abolished after independence, and as the boys grew older they went to him for permissions to visit friends or see the occasional movie. One evening he discovered Nazir jerking off, sitting in bed by himself, a magazine in front of him, caught him at just that moment of ecstatic release, and with a crushing sneer upon his face gave his son a resounding slap and picked up the magazine with two fingers and took it away to deposit in the garbage. The humiliation, the sneer. No word exchanged between father and son.

Perhaps it was the humiliation that scarred their relationship forever thereafter. Why Nazir could not draw into himself to feel pity for his father; why he could not sit down and exchange a five-minute banter with the old man and bless his day, his entire week, the short remainder of his life, with a shot of happiness.

The garden care people had come, as had the swimming pool maintenance gang; both had left calling cards and bills. A few telephone messages from Zafira's friends; a family friend with an invitation to a qawali concert at his home. Nazir was famished, ordered Chinese takeout. Before that he had a quick swim; had to watch his heart. The delivery boy came to the back, to the pool area, where he was drying himself, whisky close by.

No word from her. He was too proud to call her family, though they should know where she was; they hadn't called at all. So is this what it was going to be: divorce. All that wealth he had accumulated, gone after, now to be divided between them. She had been his partner, and that's what the law required. Though he had perhaps shortened his life a few years chasing opportunities. And he would go on chasing them with half the capital. She could relax with her portion, no worry, no heartburn, no high blood pressure. But she wouldn't know how to spend it; she would waste it away on her brothers; and she didn't know how to have fun. The initiatives in that department too had been his: where to go on holiday, where and what to eat today, which club to join; hell, what decor to put in the house.

Sitting by the pool, he thought about the Indian woman he was evicting on Danforth, who had said to him "we are as one." Her face was familiar, she must be from Dar; she would be his age, he guessed, but looked much older. Years in the new country had done nothing for her looks, her clothes, her demeanour. Where was her husband? Dead, or more likely he had left her. That woman must have been unhappy from day one, as soon as she reached maturity ... at home perhaps looking after younger siblings and cooking while parents struggled with their livelihood; given away in a doubtful marriage in the hope of some stroke of luck somewhere; husband was probably a drunkard or a gambler, visited whores on the side ... beat her up. ... All that, Nazir thought, he had seen on her face ... a frantic unhappiness, grasping at mercies.

He brooded over that face for a while, gazing into the amber in his glass that was so much a solace lately. He decided to call up his manager tomorrow and tell him to move the woman into one of the renovated apartments, her family having paid off a year's rent in advance. She would be his charge from now on.

The Expected One

The man looked sinister, exotic, as if materialized from some nightmare, some dark reach of the mind. Shirtless and grimy, he was sitting cross-legged on the ground, his back straightened against the cement wall of the station behind him. There was a red caste mark on his forehead, under his red turban. And in front of him in a basket lay a thick snake, coiled, motionless. Nagji looked away and quickly back again, a tingle creeping down his neck as he met the thin smile, the gleaming black eyes of the man.

It was hot and dusty that day in May; buses were everywhere, docked in the station, or clogging the streets outside, in various stages of departure to or arrival from destinations in Gujarat and beyond. When Nagji arrived from one of the guest houses nearby, where he had spent the night, a gang of children and a couple of emaciated women had come rushing forward to meet him, begging, pushing past each other to be closest to him. He had turned away from beseeching looks, outstretched hands, with a look of impatience, quite aware that his own eyes had betrayed his guilt and pity, which was why he was their target. At that point, quite against his will he was drawn to the snake man. There was another basket beside the snake's, in which people had dropped coins. Nagji was revolted by the snake, the worship it suggested, yet he couldn't keep his eyes averted from the dormant reptile, and the repulsive character behind it; and he couldn't walk away. The man grinned at him. Give to the deva, give to the god and he will bless, he said. Nagji took out a five-rupee note and went and dropped it into the donation basket. His heart was pounding, he intended to get away as soon as he had dropped the money. He had never been this close to a snake before, ordinarily he would be terrified. Something detained him, however, and the man began to utter a blessing. Nagji crouched in order to hear him out.

The snake stirred, sent a lazy ripple through its coiled body.

"The deva is very happy with you," the man said.

Nagji stared at the snake, the head thinner than the body, the gleaming naked eyes.

"Stroke the deva, he likes it."

Nagji lifted a hand, leaned forward: hesitantly, fearfully, drawn on. On the snake's back, up and down, he ran his hand, in small gentle strokes against the muscular brown-grey surface, rough one way, smooth the other, and with a part of his mind ready at any moment to jump up and make his escape.

The man suddenly picked up the snake with both hands, uncoiling it as he did so, his right hand just beneath the head—and Nagji fell backward, caught himself upon his hands.

Here, the man said, hold the deva, after all you are his disciple, na—

And Nagji was holding the snake, one hand under the head, the other supporting its belly, the man slowly letting go of the lower portion which was swishing gently, and the snake slowly moving its body around Nagji's, caressing his back and arm, though he never could recall later what thoughts went through his mind, or even how much time passed as he held the snake in his hands. He would retain a picture of the snake's black eyes holding his, and the sound of someone speaking in a raspy voice, as if scolding the snake man, who then gently relieved him of the reptile. As he got up on his feet he was dizzy, most likely from having been in a crouching position so long, and he was aware of the brilliant glare of the sun, and of the dust, and of the noise of people and buses. Someone was holding him up. The beggars had gone away.

He had a drink of ice-cold orange soda at a booth and contemplated the prospect ahead of him that day, aware uneasily that people were staring at him. He was on his way to his ancestral village of Be-raja, the name meaning "two kings," some twenty-five miles out of Jamnagar, this dusty metropolis at which he had arrived yesterday afternoon. There, in that village, he hoped to find an uncle; and perhaps, too, he would find a bride to his liking.

The snake man covered his charge with a lid and, carrying his two baskets in a sack, started walking. When he passed Nagji at the drink stand he put his load down and joined his hands in a gesture of salutation, without quite turning. Nagji, taken aback, attempted likewise, standing up straight, his hands around the soda bottle.

A man in his twenties, dressed in clean but worn clothes—black pants and white shirt—came over and said, "I understand you've been inquiring about Be-raja."

"Yes," Nagji said, "I'm taking a bus there."

"The only bus that goes there leaves early in the morning," the man said. "But I'm going there myself, you can come with me." Nagji hesitated, observed that the man was about as tall as he was, which was average, though he looked more stolid and a couple of years older. "Do you have a car?" he asked, before realizing the folly of the question.

"No, but we can take a bus to my village, called Bhola; from there it's a short distance, and we'll go on my motorbike."

Nagji followed.

"I'm a teacher," the man said, "every Wednesday I go to the villages around Be-raja to teach the kids. There are no schools in the area. I live in Jamnagar now, but I keep my motorbike in the village, it's easier that way." His name was Amin.

~

"I really believe," Nagji said, while in the midst of telling his story many years later in Toronto, "that my ancestors in India must have been snake worshippers; that man in the bus station, and myself, we must have been related by our previous births. I remember that in Africa my mother always spoke respectfully of snakes; once when a cobra was reported in the vicinity where we lived, for a few days she would put out a bowl of milk under the lemon tree just outside of our house. This story I heard from my older brother and sisters, it happened when I was a mere toddler, when I would go and play under that lemon tree. My mother, as you know"—Nagji said this rather matter-of-factly—"was up to all sorts of strange things."

He was talking to his real estate agent who was also the mukhi, the head of his mosque, during one of their drives around looking for a suitable house in the Thornhill area of Toronto. He was relating the story of how once he had become a holy man in India. The mukhi recalled Nagji's mother as an eccentric who used to mutter to herself as she walked, a mannerism attributed sometimes to an advanced spirituality. Nagji's father on the other hand had been ordinary, neither the silent type nor the overly gregarious, but simply ordinary, a broker of some sorts dealing in clothing merchandise.

"But we don't believe in snakes," the mukhi said, looking at Nagji sceptically. "That's primitive superstition."

"But before we became Muslims"—Nagji asserted—"if our ancestors believed in snakes, those beliefs must still be true, don't you think?"

"Perhaps," the mukhi said, thinking to himself: What do I know? If you keep faith in a snake or an elephant or a turtle, perhaps that's all that counts.

~

A few villagers of Bhola saw the bus's thick cloud of dust recede with the groan of the engine into the distance, leaving in the wake two figures of men, who then came hurrying down the path from the highway. As they neared the village, a small crowd of men and children had already gathered outside to greet them. When they were close enough to the crowd, Amin hastened forward, ahead of his companion, who took the cue and slowed down, then stopped and watched. Amin had a long chat with the men, some of whom would look up to stare at the visitor. Most of them were barefoot and dressed rather shabbily in dhotis and singlets. They all spoke softly, not a sound escaped to reach Nagji. Amin finally finished and came and said to Nagji, "Why don't you rest awhile before going on to Be-raja?" "All right," Nagji said. "They want you to bless their houses," Amin explained. "All right," the visitor replied again, nonchalantly, knowing that elders resorted to all manner of formal flattery toward strangers. "Come," said Amin, and Nagji followed.

As they arrived at the village entrance, which was a gap between two perpendicular rows of dwellings, men and women suddenly came forward and respectfully kissed Nagji's hands and touched his feet. He was embarrassed and startled, these were not children bowing to him but men and women as old as his parents. As quickly as he could he disentangled himself, pulling his hands back and stepping forward with resolve. In the company of a few men he toured the village, stopping at the houses, all of them very meagre and dark inside, and sometimes laid out with mats. At one of them he sat outside to rest, and was brought water in a glass, then sweet milk to drink from a saucer. He was mildly surprised that nothing to eat was forthcoming. The men were curious about him, and he told them what he suspected Amin had already spread around. He was from Africa, and one of his grandfathers had emigrated from Be-raja. They informed him that some of their people too had gone to Africa long ago. Before Nagji left, he was brought the village's children to bless. This he did the only way he knew how, by running a hand over their heads.

On Amin's motorcycle they raced along a back route, on a path that ran between parched fields. "The rains have failed!"—Amin called out over the bike's roar—"you've come at the right time!" "Yes," shouted back Nagji, confounded. Why was a drought the right time? Perhaps he had not heard right. They hadn't seen a soul since they left Bhola. The track brought them to a dry road upon which they blazed a trail of dust, slowing down only when they reached a handful of men and women digging inside a ditch. The diggers looked up with the barest curiosity, returned greetings with a similar enthusiasm. They were covered in dust and looked old, and remarkably there seemed nothing to dig for. "Government assistance,"

Amin explained to Nagji, "the men and women get paid simply for digging!"

Past this weird sight they came upon a sudden burst of greenery—a good-sized fenced area with leafy mango and other trees, outside a large house painted white. "Some fifteen years ago, a relation of these people came visiting from Africa, and since then he has been sending money to them," Amin explained, having slowed down. "And the others— have their relations also visited?" "No, but they are hopeful." This oasis lay at the edge of Be-raja, and no sooner had they passed it than they reached a junction from which a cart track headed off for the village. Amin dropped him off here, saying, "I have to go further to where I have to teach today, Be-raja is just up the track ahead."

Nagji started slowly walking. The sky was blue, the sun blazed down. His handkerchief was wet and ragged, he ran it again around the inside of his collar. His brow dripped like a tap. He was thirsty, and so he stopped, removed his bottle of water from his backpack and took a long drink. The yellow track, powdery under his feet, went up a slow incline between the oasis to one side and sparse scrubland to the other. Finally, beyond the summit and behind a mound of dried shrubbery, he had arrived outside the village. A group of some twenty men, women, and children had gathered, expecting him. They must have heard the motorbike.

A thin garland of wilted flowers was put around his neck by one of the men; he was given a glass of sweet milk. As he moved forward some women greeted him with a shower of rice. Such respect and devotion for a returning native!

"I've come to see Jivraj Bhai," he said to the men around him. A diminutive, scrawny man shuffled closer to him, his hands joined respectfully: "I am Jivraj." He was, Nagji had been told at home, his father's cousin. Somehow Jivraj was pushed aside and Nagji understood that a hierarchy was in place and he was in the hands of the elders.

The women were in saris and the men wore dhotis round the waist, singlets on top. All were barefoot. In a slow procession of men, Nagji was escorted inside the village to the house of the head man or mukhi, a mud structure like the others but finished with cement. He was invited to sit outside on the raised porch with some of the men to await the mukhi; others stood in a huddle at a distance, watching and listening. Above the main doorway of the house hung a few old and dusty framed photographs. The people in them reminded Nagji of his grandparents.

It took some time for the mukhi to appear; when he did, at the doorway, he looked bathed, shaved, and combed, and he wore slippers. For some moments he appraised Nagji from where he stood. Then he stepped out, space was made for him, and he sat down, facing his guest.

"We are so glad you've come," the mukhi said in a soft, even voice. His name was Hirani. The men around him nodded and murmured agreement. The mukhi added, "The visit of a returning native has been foretold since ancient times; many have left this village, and a few have returned; but you seem to be the one we have expected."

Nagji looked at the mukhi, befuddled. He didn't know how to reply. He explained instead, "My grandfather left Be-raja some seventy years ago."

Hirani and the men nodded.

"Are there more of my relations in the village besides Jivraj?" Nagji asked.

"No," the mukhi said. "But aren't we all your relatives?"

"Yes," Nagji replied, "that is true."

They were summoned for food, and a few men ate with the guest inside the house, which was a single room with a corner kitchen. The meal was exceedingly simple: a vegetable curry and a daal without much taste, with rice. The vegetables had been mashed in the cooking and were individually indiscernible; they had apparently been grown outside, in the shadow of the raised porch, between houses.

A young man came in and said to Hirani that Murad Bhai had come and was waiting outside.

"Murad Bhai, come and join us," Hirani called out, though there were scant remains in the pans and the women had yet to eat.

"I've eaten," came Murad Bhai's jovial voice.

"You will stay at the Big House," the mukhi informed Nagji. "Murad Bhai will take you there. It is his house."

There was a tamarind tree a short distance from the mango tree in the enclosed garden of the Big House. It reminded the young man of similar trees near his home in Africa, except that this one had the look of the original thing, with a thick straight stem, thick glistening leaves, and fat tamarind pods dangling alluringly from the branches. On his first morning at the House, after a short walk he went and sat down in its shade, leaning his back against its trunk. He had been given a white dhoti to wear, which he found perfect for the heat. As he sat contemplating the scenery—the bits of green close at hand and the parched brown and yellow beyond—he felt a sense of great calmness. His worries were far behind him now, across the ocean.

Having finished school, Nagji had worked for three years with his father. He expected to get married, but when the neighbours' girl whom he had always known and liked married someone else, Nagji would not consider another match. He became depressed and turned into a bit of a loner. And so his father suggested that he go to India, look up their relation, and inquire about the family property. He could also try to find a bride. And so here he was in his homeland, where people spoke his language, in exactly the same manner as his mother and father did. They had accepted him so readily, though they were perhaps too effusive in the manner in which they showed this.

Nagji had forgotten to say his prayers that morning; now, his legs crossed under him, he closed his eyes and quickly, by rote, recited them in his mind. When he opened his eyes, he was startled to see a small group of people standing outside the wire fence of the garden, staring at him. Among them were his relation Jivraj and Hirani the mukhi. When they saw him staring back at them, they joined their hands in greeting. Nagji greeted them likewise, as was appropriate. But then, to his amazement, the men entered the garden through the gate and proceeded in deliberate and careful steps toward him, and went down on their knees and bowed low before him, touching their heads to the ground.

"We knew you were the guru promised to us," Hirani said.

Unwilling to offend those who were his elders, after all, and a little flattered too by their respect, he resolved to play along until time came for him to depart. Slowly, people began to trickle by where he sat, out of respect and from curiosity. They expected to hear him, and so he spoke to them about East Africa: the cities there, the Indians in them, their occupations. The villagers had little idea of the world, except that everything was wonderful elsewhere, while here they were forlorn and forgotten. Over the years, in the past, people had left here and gone far away, crossed the seas to go to Burma and Singapore, Oman, Muscat, Zanzibar and the east coast of Africa; some would return for a bride, a very few others to stay; but gradually those visits had stopped, and for years there would be barely a word from overseas. Those who remained were left with the droughts to face, and increasing hopelessness. The young visitor told them about hardships where he came from, but those were nowhere near what his hosts had always experienced, as they very well knew—hadn't he afforded the voyage back from all that distance across the sea? Their world had not merely stood still for fifty years and more, it had actually degenerated.

The young man, before setting off for India, had imagined he was going back to the fount of his essence, where peasants were simple and joyful, the women voluptuous and melodic, as in the Indian films; where people had honest, simple values and were spiritual; and from where, when at last he had reached his ancestral village, he would learn the meanings behind all those confusing sectarian practices of faith and ritual and tradition that he had been brought up with. He had found the village; but the people he had discovered turned out to know less than he, who had grown up in a largely prosperous community, and gone daily to a large house of worship with its set and abundant routines. And so he taught them what he knew. In their ramshackle mosque in the evening, he recited hymns for them that they had not heard; he told them the history of their sect that they had long forgotten. He was giving them sermons, not in the haranguing ways he had heard in his childhood, but in the plain manner of a conversation.

One afternoon as he sat at his favourite place, Jivraj recited all the woes that had befallen him. To obtain medical treatment for his partly blinded son, he might have to sell the family plot of land and travel to Bombay. How would he earn a living in the big city? Would he be able to return to his wife and other children? What use was a life that involved so much struggle?

Jivraj had spoken a few times of inviting Nagji home, but was perhaps too embarrassed to have him there. Nagji had met his wife with a young boy one evening in the village; the woman had looked old and pathetic. In better times, she said, she would sell roasted peanuts at the bus stand on the highway; now there was nothing to sell. Nagji had put a few rupees in her boy's hand.

Now Nagji found himself telling his uncle that one's struggles were what gave meaning to one's life; success or defeat were God's to decide. And much else on the virtues of struggle. He wasn't exactly sure what he meant, it was simply a homily from his childhood and youth; the type of piety he recalled not too long ago having scorned. Jivraj, unshaved and barefoot, clothed almost in rags, heard him out, and then his face lighted up and he left.

From that day onward it became the practice that every morning as he sat under his tamarind tree, a stream of people would come to bring before him their personal woes, and he would give them the sort of advice he had given his relation Jivraj.

The drought was unending and food scarce. Most of the single young men had gone away to the city to become roadside hawkers; one or two young women too had gone away, though this was mentioned with greater embarrassment. There was one functioning well in the village, used by all to tend the tiny patches that fed the people. At dusk the houses turned quiet, huddled into their shadows; a few oil lamps flickered outside, with men gathered on a porch to chat or play cards. The women might stand at their doorways to watch or talk quietly with a neighbour. Only the insects and the children seemed oblivious to the hopelessness about; the insects chirping cheerily away in the night, the children with their games of hide-and-seek and tag in the dark, and cricket with cloth balls in the daytime. In the mornings, twice a week, they could be heard in their classroom reciting the alphabet after their teacher Amin, reciting the times tables, or singing the national anthem or a song in praise of Gandhi-ji.

Over the days and weeks the visitor came to believe in his authority and inspiration. How many were there, after all, who could claim to have brought such comfort and hope to their own people? There was the prophecy about the return of a native. And there was that incident in the city with the snake god. He felt a deeper empathy with the village; he was its saviour.

A child was born and he was asked to name it; and then another. An old man asked to be blessed before he died.

One morning as he sat down under the tree with a banana, as he was about to peel it, a hand reached out from behind and snatched it from him. The creature bounded away from his reach and, brazenly standing in front of him, finished peeling the fruit and ate it with all the time in the world. It was a female monkey. A band of monkeys had recently started invading the nearby mango tree; Nagji's first reaction to these invaders was to see them as pests and thieves. He kept a stick to ward them off, but the banana thief made it a practice to pay him a visit every afternoon, sitting some distance away, grooming herself and minding her babies, watching him curiously. He became used to her, called her Kanta Behn, after a querulous neighbour back home. Sometimes he gave her food, which she accepted with dignity and shared with her brood. He began to talk to her and it seemed to him, and to the others who watched him, that he could communicate with the monkey.

One day Kanta Behn and a friend performed a virtuoso thieving feat that left the guru gaping. Chappatis were being prepared by a maid in the kitchen of the Big House. First, Kanta Behn's friend started showing her face at the window of the kitchen, shoving her arms through the bars, and making a lot of threatening noises.

The maid finally went out to chase away the monkey, and in that short time Kanta Behn, who had been lurking on the other side of the door, dashed in and came away with the prize. When the maid raced after Kanta Behn, the friend loped into the kitchen in a few big strides and came out also with a fresh chappati. Kanta Behn stood before the amused Nagji, utterly composed, ready to eat her chappati. But then she tore it in two and presented one half to a grateful Nagji.

Nagji knew now that he utterly belonged. Not only the snake god but also the monkey god had accepted him.

A village couple had invited him for dinner and to bless their childless home. The hovel was no worse than most he had seen by now, but it had a pile of rubble in one corner that let off a dank, unpleasant odour. A supply of cement had apparently been ordered but not arrived. The meal was village fare, which he ate with the man, Raju, while he delivered his usual homilies about struggle and faith. Raju's wife served them when required, otherwise stood by in the shadows. She was not much older than him, Nagji observed in the yellow light of the kerosene lamp, as she bent over them to serve, and her face was flushed. She was in sari, the threadbare blouse stretched tight across her breasts. Her husband Raju sat up straight, legs crossed, watching an uncomfortable but hungry guest eat; he was tall and rather sombre-looking, with a long unshaven face and an almost bald head.

After they had eaten, the two men went to sit outside in darkness for a while, and between awkward silences Nagji learned that Raju went every day to hawk plastic

jewellery on the highway from a cart that he rented. His
wife came from a group of five villages, a day's bus ride
away. He had relations in the city of Rajkot.

When finally Nagji asked permission to leave, Raju
said, "I want one more favour from you, guru-ji."

"If I can do it, it's yours," the guru told him. He was
touched by the man's quiet dignity, preserved amidst
such extremely humble circumstances.

"I would like you to bless my wife's womb, if you will,
please."

The young guru was not prepared for this, whatever it
meant. "I will bless both you and your wife," he said after
a pause, "may you have—"

"Come, guru-ji," Raju said, standing up, and the two
men went inside, where the wife sat beside the lamp,
whose wick had been lowered to give the barest illumina-
tion. Raju muttered something to her and left, and Nagji
unexpectedly found himself alone with the woman, his
heart beating insistently inside him. She was on a sleeping mat, one leg folded under her, the other partly
stretched forward. She had been combing her hair. Some
stale flowers were spread out on a small pillow; there was
the odour of hair oil, a whiff of burning incense.

"Come," Kulsum said in a quivering voice, taking his
hand, and the young guru went along with her guidance,
all defences vanquished, hostage to his virility and a child
in her arms. He went to bless her womb two more times,
after which it was understood he was no longer required,
and he was racked with guilt and confusion. He was chosen, but surely not to bestow blessings in such a carnal
manner; to be the recipient of such a trust from simple

men and women seemed extravagant and wrong. He had actually enjoyed himself, melting into that dark body with its odour of musty spice and just plain flesh; looking forward to the next day, and the next. And the woman had received him with evident pleasure. He had only once coupled with a woman before, had hardly been aware of what transpired. Now, initiated, could he ever look upon the women with innocence, as a teacher, a saviour?

He convinced himself that the episode had been pre-ordained: as a test and a warning to him to beware of temptation. He had after all not chosen to be what he had become.

A year had passed since he first arrived. His skin had darkened from exposure, his beard and hair had grown. A few sparse but welcome rains had fed the parched earth and were duly attributed to his blessed arrival. Raju and his wife had a baby son whom the guru named Rahim. He was required to visit several of the nearby villages now, to which he was taken by the teacher Amin on the motorbike. But the condition of the people remained what it had always been.

One morning at about eleven a taxi arrived, an elegant cream-coloured Ambassador with blue curtains in the side windows to keep the sun out. From it emerged a fat middle-aged man wearing a shirt suit of the same colour as the car, and sunglasses. His name was Ali Jadavji and he came from Africa. He was accorded the same welcome as the young guru had received a year before. This was reported to the guru by his relation Jivraj as he sat under his tamarind tree. Over the months Jivraj had, unasked, assumed the role of an usher, while also ministering to Nagji's needs. Thus Jivraj had acquired some prestige in the village. Nagji now told him he was tired, to answer Jivraj's concern regarding the new arrival, though he was actually also worried. Jivraj fetched a cup of tea for him from the Big House before he left.

That afternoon a large group of men came by to see him. In the middle and prominent among them by his size and evident well-being was the new visitor. The gate to the enclosure was opened and the men came through and stood some ten feet away from the guru. Most of them joined hands respectfully, but the visitor in the shirt suit, uncomfortable and sweaty, declined to do so, sizing him up sceptically instead.

"May I know your good name, Brother," Ali Jadavji asked.

"I have shed my name and the world with it," the guru replied astutely. But he could barely keep his voice steady. For he recognized the man as a prominent trader from his hometown.

"Guru Nameless then," Ali Jadavji smiled grimly, and after a moment's hesitation he turned around to leave. The entourage left with him.

The man knew him, of that Nagji had hardly a doubt. But how? Had he been recognized so easily, almost instantly, behind his beard and hair and emaciated frame? Nagji now recalled a scene from the past, when he used to be one of the ragamuffins who would play marbles in the grounds of the town mosque in Dar es Salaam every evening, until they were dispersed at prayer time. Ali Jadavji had been one of the men sitting outside on the stone benches, watching the dusty-kneed boys getting chased toward the water taps, and commenting on their worthless pedigrees.

Nagji realized that afternoon that his calling, or dream, or charade—what *was* it?—was now over.

That evening as he emerged from the village prayer hall—alone, for Mr. Jadavji had gathered around him all the attention, with his authority and bearing and signs of wealth—Jivraj fell into step beside him and told him: "This Jadavji, whoever he is, has called you a nobody from Dar es Salaam and a fake, and Hirani the mukhi and others are paying attention to him . . . and that Raju is saying really bad shameless things about you—"

Early the next morning Nagji begged a ride from the teacher Amin and headed for the nearest bus stop.

~

As the Toronto mukhi, who was also a real estate agent, showed Nagji a house that finally interested him—it was one of those large modern residences that are all the fashion among wealthy immigrants, with imposing facades that remind you of mansions in Beverly Hills, except they all look identical and are densely packed in a development—he observed to himself that Nagji was, like many others he knew, prone to exaggeration if not exactly the tall tale. Nagji's story did not lack its details, some of them no doubt rendered more colourful with the passage of time. Perhaps Kanta Behn the monkey had acquired a more prominent role now, in memory's generous version; perhaps she had been named Shanta Behn or Kadak Bai, or given no name at all. And perhaps the guru's tree was a guava tree, or even something nondescript and small. And the snake?—who could tell, but the *nag* in Nagji's name did mean "cobra." The whole story certainly could be the gist of a humorous novel about India.

Nagji had, a few years after that first visit, returned to Be-raja and fetched his son Rahim, who had grown up in Canada and was now a strapping youth of eighteen, playing basketball and planning to study computers at Waterloo. Seeing him, and especially hearing him speak, you would never place him in a desperate, drought-ridden village in Gujarat.

Ali Jadavji, well known in the Ontario community, lives coincidentally in Waterloo as well and is ailing. He had been a widower when he arrived that fateful day in the Indian village, looking for a wife. Nagji's father's tales, back in Dar, of his son's reception in the ancestral village, had prompted Ali's interest in the place, and that's where he went to pick a wife. He came away with a seventeen-year-old girl, whose family no doubt felt privileged at being able to free their daughter from the crushing poverty. That girl, now a woman in her thirties, has left her husband and sponsored her family's immigration to Canada. Meanwhile the villages outside Jamnagar have prospered from the attentions of all the young people going back to search for their roots. And so the guru perhaps was a blessing of sorts during the years of drought and need.

Her Two Husbands

How ironic for him, she thought,
that it began with a phone call, the unravelling of his
presence in her life. He had said to her once, "Yasmin, if
someone were to sweet-talk to you on the phone and
convinced you to do it, you would smother one of your
own children." Not fair, that taunt, it stung. But it was
true that she was easy to take advantage of sometimes,
because she found it hard to be abrupt with people, was

loath to seem cold and rude to them. Once or twice something *had* got burnt on the stove because of the phone; and how many times had she been wheedled into a purchase or a donation she regretted as soon as she put the receiver down. But now he was dead and it was precisely the phone which had brought to her her new husband, and a new, more love-filled life.

It was almost a year since Aseema at the office had cornered her one day with an invitation, saying, "There's a mushaira this weekend at Abid Bhai's—why don't you come, yaar, it should be a lot of fun." Yasmin, smiles and apologies, had declined, but Aseema persisted: "Step out of your weeds, sweetheart, come and meet the world; you do have a life to lead, you know." Yasmin said she would think about it, and Aseema had gone away looking pleased with herself.

Yasmin had no intention of going to the function. It was all right to go unescorted where people knew you well, or even sometimes where they were completely alien. But Pakistanis, Aseema's people, seemed familiar and yet also alien, and always so very formal and conservative . . . she would not at all feel comfortable among them.

Aseema herself was far from conservative in her manner; she made herself up with dabs of mascara and other eye stuff and dark purple lipstick spread thickly on her wide lips, and with her open-mouthed smile and half-closed eyes she could turn on a lascivious look to excite even the younger men who worked with her and Yasmin. But she was an exception. She had been to exclusive private schools in Pakistan, with American teachers and all that, a fact she never failed to stress if there was ever the slightest chance of her being taken for a regular "Paki." The invitation she had brought Yasmin was to a private Urdu poetry recital at her brother Abid's house. Over the years Aseema had extended several such invitations to Yasmin and Karim; and over the years Karim had pooh-poohed the very idea of an Urdu mushaira in Toronto, and put his wife off it too.

Yasmin had married a grim-natured man. Loving, yes, and passionate, too; but opinionated, for he was a widely read professor, and dark in outlook. *Dark* was the word; she had gotten used to watching ruefully as that telltale shadow came over his face, from its first appearance as a blank look in the eyes to the flush spreading across the cheeks, when some particularly sensitive issue, political or moral, came up. Regardless of the occasion, you only had to wait for the eruption—the barely controlled statement of opinion, and then gradually the furious torrent. He'd grown darker and angrier with age as he saw the world slip away from him, and himself become an old fogey to a new generation of young professors at work, to the young people he met, to the young women he saw.

What Urdu culture, he'd say scornfully. Do their children even *speak* Urdu anymore, let alone read or write Urdu poetry? Inviting an Urdu-wallah from Pakistan or India to give a mushaira does not make the growth of Urdu literature in Canada. And how long can one go on hearing about the moth consumed in the flame of love, and the tender-cheeked rose weeping dewdrops at dawn. . . .

He was exaggerating, of course, even as he made flowing gestures with his right hand in imitation of Urdu poets, and he knew it. He had perfected damning scorn to a fine art. He was too learned for his own good. The truth was that he had given up on Indian-Pakistani culture as of no significance to his life in the West; to him it was the transplanted variety we had here, superficial and mediocre. Why not give up the game, he would say, and pay attention to what's authentic and around us?

A day or two after Aseema's invitation, her brother Abid had called.

"Yasmin," he said, "you know why I am calling."

"No . . . well . . ." and she gave a little laugh. She had met Abid once when he came to see his sister at work, and she remembered him as an excessively polite and quite handsome man.

"What a pleasant laugh," he said. "Seriously, you've made my day already. Listen, Yasmin, aren't you interested even a little in Urdu poetry? It's our culture, after all—"

"I am," she said hesitantly. Like many people, she enjoyed listening occasionally to ghazals sung to music, she even had a collection on a CD somewhere. But she didn't know much else about Urdu poetry, except the name of the most famous poet Ghalib, about whom she'd seen a popular Indian film. Aseema had told her about the others, but she couldn't quite remember their names. Iqbal? Faiz?

"I am calling to invite you personally, Yasmin. Gharib Ferangi—yes, his name rhymes with *Ghalib*, isn't that funny? And Gharib—yes, that name means 'poor'!— Ferangi is *the* most important poet in Urdu today. . . ."

Important according to whom?—she heard her dead husband's voice at the back of her head, imagined that scornful face behind her, as usual to the point and giving no quarter.

Abid's voice on the phone was melodious, respectful, and full of humility. If the consensus had ruled that Gharib Ferangi was the most important Urdu or Pakistani poet alive, he wouldn't be the one to argue the point.

"Only the most select people will be there, I assure you," he went on, "sophisticated people, not intrusive and not religious—I know that worries you. We all are not fundamentalists, and if you read some of Ferangi's poetry it will make you blush. He has even had some fatwas issued against him!"

She was trapped, what could she do? As Karim would say, The house may burn down, but you couldn't say to the person at the other end: lay off; no, I can't do it; I'm not buying; whatever.

"I really am not sure," she replied, to Abid.

"It's only a cultural evening," Abid insisted, "a party, and we want the most diverse and enlightened group, Yasmin. . . ."

The critical voice in her mind she managed to squeeze out, and she said, "Let me call you back. I'll have to check with the children and their plans."

"Please do so," Abid said. "Of course you should, you are a mother. And thank you. I know you will enjoy yourself."

You did it again, the voice said. She had tears in her eyes.

*

Abid was right. When she went to the mushaira-party at his house in Mississauga, she enjoyed herself thoroughly. The poet Ferangi was a short, balding man, wearing white kurta-pyjama and black waistcoat, and what a voice! He was given the place of honour, the wide sofa in the living room, his adulating audience gathered before him on the broad-loomed floor. They were all familiar with his works, having studied them in college back in Pakistan. He would recite from their requests, and frequently they would sponta-neously join in, in a happy chorus, and finish the last lines of a poem with him. He was a charming man, funny and profound; at times he stood up to recite, at times he sang, in the traditional posture, his left arm at his waist and his right arm before him performing for the audience. There would be back-and-forth banter, and behind every poem would be a spellbinding story. There was a break for dinner, which was a buffet with an immense variety of meat dishes. The poet was indulged with a glass and a bottle of Glenfiddich placed before him reverently where he sat. No one else drank alcohol. Yasmin was disappointed that Aseema had not come, but she was treated with a lot of respect and affection. The women, mostly sitting close together inti-mately, were warm in their manner, and looked lovely in saris and shalwar kameez. They listened to Ferangi's some-times risqué pronouncements, casually delivered, about his or other poets' affairs, about genitalia or excrement, with the utmost composure. The poet had apparently picked his themes from his memories of life in the small town in India in which he had grown up. Yasmin made that observation to him and he expounded upon it. I was right to have come, she said both to herself and to the absent Karim. And all

Urdu poetry is not about candles and moths, the rose and the early-morning dew, and "gham."

And where does Ferangi live now? he retorted. England. And was there anyone under forty at the meeting? QED.

But no, QED or not, she had won the day. She had started to go out, and that was good.

Abid called her to thank her for coming—"for condescending to grace us with your presence," was how he put it.

"What do you mean, 'condescending'? It was such a wonderful opportunity to meet a genuine, living Urdu poet! Thank *you* for inviting me."

"You are most welcome," he told her. "You were truly a blessing there."

Typical Urdu flattery, said that voice in her mind, typical India-Pakistan—even when a dagger is being thrust at your back, in front is all honeyed talk, You first, *aap pahele*, please, there's no one such as your gracious self, all 'umble Uriah Heep—

You're jealous! she retorted.

A couple of weeks later Aseema said to Yasmin, in her usual manner, "You know, sweetie pie, I believe brother Abid is smitten with you—don't tell me I haven't warned you, kiddo."

For the next few days Yasmin's nerves were on tenterhooks. What to do? What to think? This was totally unexpected, she was completely unprepared for it. Then Abid called.

"How are you?"

"Fine," she answered, "but don't tell me another Urdu event is coming up so soon!"

"No . . . well there is, but that's not why I called. I would like to take you to a concert, of the Toronto Symphony—you do like Western classical?"

"Yes, up to a point, I'm not really an expert—"

"Neither am I—"

"And I can't stand the modern stuff."

Which Karim would sometimes take her to, saying, Listen with the mind sometimes, Yas, these days even the hip-hoppers are humming Beethoven's Ninth—

"Neither can I," Abid told her. "This is an all-Beethoven concert, with the Ninth Symphony, and it is my favourite!"

She hesitated. Was it right? Was this a date? What did Abid expect of her? There was a moment's silence while she quickly reflected and he let her.

Then he said, "I had two tickets given me by a client and I thought you might like to come. It's discreet, our people don't usually go to these events—though I believe your late husband did. You know he was highly respected in our Asian communities, though I didn't quite agree with some of his comments—he struck me as . . . angry." He caught himself and said, "Come on, Yasmin, I'm quite harmless, really—"

She laughed, and she agreed to go.

And so eventually she agreed to marry him; and the ghost of Karim, if there was one, became a glowering bitter face in the background, occasionally erupting but more often silent.

What she liked about Abid's people, his community—which consisted of friends and some near and distant relatives—was their gentility, the grace and respect they showed to each other. Of course this was only external form and etiquette; nevertheless, she realized that she had never been accorded such treatment before. In return she lived up to the expectations implicitly demanded of her. She now wore the sari or shalwar kameez, attires which she liked very much, with all their colour and grace, though there was the odd occasion when she sensed a qualm within herself and wished she had the pluck to look different—come out for instance in a khaki skirt and red tank top, or (God forbid) shorts, during summer. At parties she was pulled toward the women, away from the men. She had already learned to defer to the elders of her new community in the formal, elaborate, and quite charming ways expected, which reminded her of the Indian movies of her childhood. She felt a bit hypocritical after such displays. Abid himself was a soft-hearted, genial sort who rarely raised his voice, which was strange for her because she had been used to shows of excitement or anger from a husband. The whole tenor of her life had become orderly and calm, if a little constrained.

You've sunk, said that voice once. Don't you have an iota of a sense of who you were, who you really are?

What was I? she retorted. *You* made me!

She and Karim had met twenty years ago when she was a new assistant librarian in the history department of the University of Toronto and he a quiet professor. Even then he exuded that darkness of soul, though she saw it only as a romantic, somewhat Keatsian trait. They got to talking once about a journal recently discontinued by the library, then about other excellent journals guillotined by university cutbacks, and over the weeks gradually became intimate. She had no doubts when she accepted to marry him. He was charming and easy to be with, vastly educated, and slightly mysterious. She liked the fact that he was westernized, refreshingly different in his thinking from what she was used to seeing in men from their background. He took her to a whole new world of the opera, music concerts, book readings and museums, the thrill of living in the city, away from the suburban developments filling up with immigrants. The kids came and put a new twist on their existence. He spurned religious education for them as a regimen cooked up by a bunch of ignorant, uncultured managers to keep their people in line. She more or less agreed, but (as she sometimes argued) what was wrong with the kids spending time with their own kind? Her reservations arose mainly because she was losing friends. They were all professionals, married to other professionals or businessmen, and all observant community members—a class Karim had contemptuously dismissed as the "Markhamites" and the "Scarberians," suburbanites spending their nonworking hours on the highways and in mosque. He was so passionate in his beliefs, she simply went along with them because ultimately she didn't quite care as much, and she wanted him happy. But she had her qualms and she had her guilt. She needed her God in small doses, like normal people.

He was, of course, a professed agnostic—all that meant was that he battled against God all the time, worried about all the problems ailing the world. What had seemed like a darkly romantic trait, a soulful detail in his character, had grown into a hopeless view of the world and an anger simmering beneath his surface. Deep in his heart, she believed, he missed being a suburbanite, happy with his people and happy in his simple, blind faith.

He always thought he would die young, and when he finally did so, in his fifties of stroke, it was almost with relief in his eyes, in all his demeanour—the world had been too much for him; and she too felt a semblance of relief, for he had made her so conscious of his impending death. But then, after he died, he started to haunt her—or, what was the same thing, she began to recall his presence. She heard his voice in her mind, felt his presence looming behind her, whenever she felt she was straying from the path the two of them had followed together.

Of their three children, the two eldest were on their own, the first, a son, working at a downtown brokerage firm, and the second, a daughter, in university in the States. The youngest, a son, was eleven and had come with her to her new life; he was reserved but polite with Uncle Abid. Her husband's attempts to teach him Urdu or interest him in the tenets of Islam had been to no avail.

Yasmin felt loved—by Abid; by his friends and their wives; by her stepdaughter Rabbia, who occasionally came to visit them with her young family and had taken an immense liking to Yasmin.

"Amma," Rabbia said, "you are an angel, you've come like a farishta into my father's life. He gave up so many years of his life out of respect for my mother, worrying about me—but you know what, the wait was worth it. I've never known him happier—*never*, if you get my meaning."

"I get your meaning, thank you," Yasmin replied, with a smile. "And I've also . . . never been happier. . . ."

Never? And that pregnant pause, that sharp breath you took there for a moment before that glib remark . . . *never?* Not when the first child, Emil, was born? Not on that trip to Acapulco, or Spain—in Andalusia, in Cordoba— that second honeymoon?

I am happy as I've never been in a long time. I am respected as a woman and a wife, not as a mere companion and sex partner. I am the lady of the house and a lady in a community. My husband is calm and gentle; he rarely gets annoyed, and I have yet to see him at full boil. He is not at war with the world, he is a meditative, a spiritual man.

Visiting Pakistan was the most wonderful event of her life. Yes, it eclipsed all those memories of Andalusia, strolling with Karim through fields of orange and bougainvillea, hand in hand staring up at the awesome ceiling of the Great Mosque in Cordoba or at the palace of Alhambra, the two of them picking up their lives again when the kids were older. Of course on this trip there was no dearth of the frustrations typical of the Third World—long waits at the airport, people jumping queues, dimwitted or sleazy officials, murderous traffic. But there was such warmth in the people she met; she had never experienced anything like it in Canada. You knew these were your people, in spite of the differences; and all the history of the country, going back two thousand years, was part of your history, too. They spent most of their time in Lahore, which was Abid's hometown. To his family, Yasmin was royalty; she was greeted by them with embraces and tears of joy, with gifts of clothing and jew- ellery. There were elaborate family feasts in her honour, she went shopping and sightseeing, was invited to private music parties with blood-curdling qawalis by the best singers—that makes you envious, doesn't it, Karim, all *authentic* and *real*, the way you wanted everything. Young women, older ones, confided in her, their new bhabhi or bahu from Canada, young men called her Auntie and teased her.

Abid had two brothers and a sister in Lahore. He also had Aseema in Toronto and another sister in Chicago. The family's business in Lahore was transportation. They also owned land. Abid's father was dead—Yasmin was taken to pay her respects at the grave—and his mother, tall and bony with grey eyes and a wonderful smile, was the matriarch to whom all paid respect. Nothing was done without consulting her. The family had a spiritual adviser, Sheikh Murad Ali, who also advised in worldly matters.

When the family took her to see the Sheikh, Yasmin had to tie a plain black scarf around her head—the Sheikh was insistent, they told her with a twinkle in their eyes, he had to be humoured. A loose dupatta, with wisps of hair blowing at the forehead, just wouldn't do in his presence. He was liable to produce a rough cloth himself and tie it firmly around your head if he didn't like your covering. He didn't care for jeans either, even on men.

He turned out to be a small-statured man with a radiant pink face and a long white beard, attired in a shimmering silk kurta of a pale colour and an embroidered cap. His cold grey eyes made her look away the first time he laid eyes on her. The walls in his study, where he received them, opening the double doors himself to let them in, were lined with books and bound manuscripts and hung in places with framed Arabic calligraphy. There was an odour of faint perfume and recent incense in the air. He bade them sit on the carpeted floor, from which a small prayer mat was first rolled away, and a large silver tray of offerings was placed before him, piled with presents—a pen and a Palm Pilot, some dried fruit, and cash in dollars—which he received without much ado. The talk soon turned to serious matters, and as his guidance to them the Sheikh warned them about Western materialism, which people everywhere in the world were blindly emulating while losing their own spiritual values. The men enjoyed discussing world politics with him, but they did this with due deference to his views. The women listened silently to this discussion or spoke to each other in whispers.

To Yasmin, the Sheikh's beliefs seemed narrow and rigid, and it was a trial of patience to keep sitting there on the floor meekly listening to them. She lost her control finally and sprung to the defence of her gender, saying, "But women are not men's property, and they are not half the worth of men." The Sheikh, at first startled into a pause, gave a look of amusement and replied, "They are worth *more* than men, Béta, that's why Murshid-ul-kameel has given us all these elaborate laws regarding men and women." Her in-laws explained to her what was meant, and Yasmin dutifully said, "Oh." But that fooled nobody.

"That's one side of Pakistan I will never accept," she said to Abid later, "this treatment of women," having told him first that she didn't think she cared too much for Sheikh Murad Ali.

That pleased Karim. Told you so, the voice said. Pakistan, he had always said, was a tragedy on the Indian subcontinent, a non-country that had never worked, never been really independent, never been democratic, was an embarrassment. He could go on and on, making judgments so sweeping, so cruel and unfair—the kinds of generalizations he would swiftly decry in others. Look what you got yourself into, he now gloated, an orthodox soup!

You are jealous, only, she replied. I have a people, a place to belong to, a culture and a faith—and you, you had zip, nothing, and that's why all your anger at the world. I have your number, Karim Bharwani, finally; I know where *you* came from, in spite of your Wagner and Beethoven, Marx and Freud—from nowhere, and how you longed for the certainty I've achieved. Even now, in death, what do you have? Have you found peace at last? No, you flit round the globe, from one disaster area to another, seeing only famine and genocide, car bombs and smart weapons, raging at the injustice and inhumanity all over. Not satisfied, you return to torment me.

It was only Karim and the Sheikh in Lahore who were the spoilers in her new life. Karim she could manage. She knew him, and he was dead, after all. But the Sheikh?

"He's an old man, Yasu," Abid assured her. "He'll soon be gone—how long do you think he will live? And his heir Salamat Ali is not so old-fashioned."

"Not so orthodox, you mean. Fundamentalist."

He laughed. "That's just a word."

"Anyway, Murad Ali looked quite healthy to me. People like that take good care of themselves, they don't die easily. And his son could turn out even worse."

"Don't *worry*," Abid said. "It's temporary, this edict. In time, Murad Ali will relent. Remember, he has our good at heart—he is our interpreter of the faith and our agent with God."

Not two months had passed since their visit to Pakistan, when the Sheikh sent the edict that came like a rock thrown at the boat that was her life. Abid was told about it by his sister, who called late one night from Lahore. He was so stunned he forgot to hide his reaction from Yasmin, who was listening and watching from the bed.

"*What?* Are you sure ... *every* woman? Even in Canada and US? Think of public relations. He won't relent? Arré what's come over him ... thik hé, then. But try. Soften him up a bit. ..."

The Sheikh had pronounced that the moral order in the world continued to decline. It pained him to see that even decent people had begun to deviate from the path of the righteous, dazzled by the attractions conjured up by wily Azazel, beguiled by honeyed words from the forked tongue of Satan. He, Sheikh Murad Ali of Lahore, was exhorting his followers to rectify their habits and come back to the path. Rules regarding halal were to be followed strictly. Personal hygiene was to be observed according to Islamic tradition. And women had to cover their heads with a black or white chador that reached at least to their shoulders.

Yasmin, shocked beyond belief, had little doubt that this edict from afar was the real answer to her outburst in the Sheikh's study in Lahore. She recalled the old man's initial reaction when she spoke up—that pause, the stillness that momentarily overcame him before he recovered with the smile and the patronizing comment. His eyes had grazed her neck, met hers, before he lightly dismissed her objection. She had met his eyes again on the way out. She felt humbled and defeated by his power over her now.

"You've betrayed me," she said tearfully to her husband. "You misled me—"

"Yasmin, my life, how can you say that?"

"You expect me to wear that . . . that tent over my head?"

"Not a *tent*—" he laughed—"it's supposed to come only to the shoulders. He's our Sheikh, my love, he stands between us and God. And it's only temporary."

My foot, she wanted to blurt out, but held her peace.

She sulked and wept intermittently all that day, and the next.

The following evening a potluck dinner was arranged at a friend's house to discuss this new edict of Sheikh Murad Ali, their leader. Ten couples were present, and to Yasmin's surprise nobody showed any concern about the ruling. A few people even poked a little fun at it and at some of the Sheikh's ways (for example, he burped loudly and with relish). What could have set him off? the question was raised. Perhaps Benazir Bhutto's recent antics. Or the recent performance of the Pakistan cricket team. Or the jokes that were made even there about President Clinton's affair with that girl Monica Lewinsky, a name familiar in every village now, following the recent TV crash course on sex. They discussed ways of bending the new rule: the Sheikh had ordered white or black chador to be worn, but he didn't specify what material, and hadn't placed any injunctions on the designs printed or embroidered on it; and surely, they agreed, black meant simply dark, therefore blue would be acceptable; the chador should reach the shoulders, but even a dupatta did that. . . . There were of course arguments among the men, as there usually were, when the subject veered off toward world politics. There was plenty of food to eat. Poetry was recited, songs were sung. Yasmin was reminded sharply of the sense of community among these people, of their common struggles against life's crazy contradictions, and the sense of humour they could always call upon to cope with them. She went home immensely relieved.

That night she and Abid spent many tender moments together. At length, when they were ready to go to sleep, he asked, "Is it too late for you to have a child?"

"I think so. Why, you want one? I could ask the doctor."

"No. . . . We are both done with that. We need all the time to be with each other and enjoy life."

"I agree."

And so, said that voice in her head, as she lay on her back, wide awake but eyes gently shut, happy, listening to her own breathing, and that of the man beside her. And so, said that voice, a smidgin of sex, a bit of *meri jaan*, and you'll go out tomorrow wearing a tent on the head—

Stop it! He loves me, and it's not a tent. You know that. . . . And what do you mean by "a smidgin of sex" anyway? He's better at it than you were by a long shot—

Oh yeah, I didn't see you exactly moaning with helpless pleasure now or screaming for more—

It's not just the moaning and screaming, you insensitive man, it's also the gentleness, the love you feel inside every pore of your entire body, the—

I see.

That takes care of him, she thought, regaining her breath. Finally. She sensed him receding from her mind . . . he would go away for ever now, truly dead. She realized all of a sudden that she didn't quite want that to happen. She began to miss him.

Karim? she called.

Yes? Sullen, and distant, as if from the door.

But I do need you . . . stay . . .

Aw, he said.

It was almost a year since Abid had come into her life.

Last Rites

"Shamshu Mukhi," she said, "how are you?"

I had just stepped out of the front doorway of the Don Mills mosque and onto the stoop, where she had been standing, waiting.

"Hale and hearty, and how is the world treating you, Yasmin," I replied jovially. The formal address *mukhi* always provokes an exaggerated, paternal sort of cheeriness in my manner that I can't quite curb and (as I've realized over the years) don't wish to either, because it is what people expect, draw comfort from. But no sooner had my glib response escaped my lips than I was reminded by her demeanour that lately the world had not been treating Yasmin Bharwani very kindly.

I asked her, more seriously: "And how is Karim—I understand he's in hospital?"

A pinprick of guilt began to nag. It was more than a week now since I heard that her husband, who had been a classmate of mine, had been admitted for something possibly serious. I had not seen Bharwani in years, our paths having diverged since we ended up in this city; still, I had meant to go and do my bit to cheer him up for old times' sake. Only, with this and that to attend to, at home and away, that good thought had simply sieved through the mind.

She nodded, paused a moment to look away, before turning back to reply, "He's at Sunnybrook. I've come to ask, can you give him chhanta? . . ."

"Now, now, Yasmin, don't talk like that. It can't be serious—he's young yet, we all are." (That irrepressible bluster again—who was I kidding, since when has the Grim Reaper given a hoot about age?) "And what will your unbelieving husband Karim say to my giving him chhanta—he will scream murder."

Chhanta is the ceremony at which a person is granted forgiveness by his mukhi on behalf of the world and the Almighty. You join hands and supplicate once a month at new moon, and then finally at death's bed. I recall a sceptical Bharwani from our boyhood days arguing with hotheaded arrogance, "What have I done against the world that I should crave forgiveness all the time?" And some of us replying, "If nothing else, you might have stepped on an ant and killed it, ulu—even an angel commits at least seven sins daily, and what do you think, that you are better than an angel?" We called him "Communist" in those teen years, which nickname he rather relished, for it had intellectual connotations and set him apart from the rest of us, all destined for the heavenly embrace.

"Try, please," his wife now begged me. "He's dying . . . and there's another matter too. . . ."

At this moment Farida joined me, and we invited Yasmin to come home and have supper with us, when she could also unburden her mind. We had anticipated a quiet Sunday evening together, but such sacrifices of privacy have been our pleasure, having brought meaning to our lives as we approach what are called our more mellow years. It is a traditional responsibility that I hold, as presider of a mosque, father to its community; nothing could seem safer for someone so conventional, indeed mediocre, as I, until Yasmin and Karim Bharwani put me through an ordeal from which I don't think I recovered.

Yasmin must be some five years younger than both my wife and I; she is petite and trim, fair complexioned, with short dark hair. She was dressed smartly that night, though perhaps a bit sternly. She had her own car, so we met in the lobby of our building and went up together. At first we discussed anything but the gloomy subject at hand, her husband's illness. Finally, over a swiftly put-together supper, an assortment of leftover and fresh, I said to Yasmin, who was waiting for just such a prompt, "Now tell us what's this other matter that you mentioned."

She looked anxiously at me and said all in a rush: "My husband wishes to be cremated when he dies."

I spluttered out a quite meaningless: "But why?" to which nevertheless she answered, "I don't know why, I don't understand his reasons—he has plenty of them and I don't understand them."

"But surely you've not given up hope yet," Farida said, "it's too soon to talk of. . . ." Her voice trailed off. We watched Yasmin break down silently, large tears flowing down her cheeks. Farida went and sat beside her, poured her a glass of water. "Pray for him," she whispered. "We will, too."

"You must come and give him chhanta . . . now," the grieving woman answered, wiping away her tears.

The three of us drove to Sunnybrook Hospital, Farida going with Yasmin in the latter's car.

Trust Karim Bharwani to pose a conundrum such as this one. Always the oddball, always the one with the dissenting opinion: why this way and not the other? Because the world is so, eh chodu, we would laugh him off. There were times when we vilified him, mercilessly, and tried to ostracize him, when he had wounded our pietistic feelings with one of his poisoned utterings. But he was too much one of us, you might as well cast out a part of your body. Now here he was, saying cremate me, don't bury me. The trouble is, we don't cremate our dead, we bury them, according to the Book, the same way Cain first disposed of his brother Abel.

I wanted to say to him, as I saw him, Look, Bharwani, this is not the time for your smart, sceptical arguments.

This is real, this is how you leave the world; at least this once, walk along with the rest of us.

He had been washed. His face was flushed, but creased, and he looked exhausted and frail. He had always had rather prominent eyes behind big black-framed glasses; now his eyeballs were sunken deep inside their sockets, where two tiny black pools of fire burned with fervid life. There was barely any flesh on the cheeks. He reminded me rather of a movie version of an extra-terrestrial. He said, in answer to his wife's concerns, that he had been taken for a short walk; yes, he had eaten a bit of the awful food, to keep his strength; and today the pain was less. He would die for a curry; he attempted a laugh. He sounded hoarse and a little high-pitched. He had let an arm drop to the side of the bed; I picked it up, cold, and squeezed it. "Ey, Bharwani, how are you?"

"It's been a long time," he said, meaning presumably the time since we last met. He smiled at Farida, who had gone and sat at the foot of the bed. "Mukhi and Mukhiani," he said to the two of us, with an ever so slight mock in his tone, "so have you come to give me chhanta?"

I threw a look at Yasmin, who turned to him with large, liquid eyes. "Let them," she pleaded. "In case. It's our tradition."

He said nothing for a moment, apparently trying to control himself. Then, in measured tones: "Doesn't it matter what I believe in or desire for myself?"

She had no argument, only the desperate words of a beloved: "For my sake. . . ."

He fell back exhausted, closed his eyes; opened them to stare at me. I saw my chance then, in that helpless look, and drove home my simple argument: "Karim, it can't hurt, whatever it is you believe in." With a laugh, I added: "Surely you don't believe you have nothing to ask forgiveness for?"

He grinned, at me, at his wife, and said, "You have a point there."

I proceeded with the ceremony, having brought the holy water. When we had finished, he joked, "I should go to heaven now."

"You *will* go to heaven," Yasmin said happily, "when the time comes. But it was only a formality now." She smiled and her look seemed to drench him in love. "And you'd not asked forgiveness from God in years."

"But I asked forgiveness from you, not from Him."

"Oh." But she was not bothered.

"But I am firm about the other thing, I tell you. I insist. These two people here are witnesses to my wish. I would like to be cremated when I die, not buried in that cold ground at Yonge and Sheppard called Immigrant's Corner."

"But why, Karim, why?" For the first time, her voice animated, passionate.

"Because I *want* it so."

"It's not right."

"What difference does it make? I'll be *dead*. Doesn't it matter to you how I want to be treated in death, what I believe in?"

She wiped away tears, looked straight at him and said, "All right. But I'll have the prayers said over you by Mukhisaheb. A proper service."

"All right, Shamshu can say his juju over my body—if they let him."

*

He knew it would not be a simple matter fulfilling his last wish. And so for him I was a godsend, a witness to that wish who had known him in the past and was not unsympathetic, and who was also a mukhi, with connections. He also used the presence of me and my wife to extract grudging acquiescence from his own wife. There the matter stood when Farida and I took leave of the couple in the dingy, eerily quiet hospital room, our footsteps echoing hollowly down the long, white corridors. We both believed there was time still, for Bharwani and Yasmin to wrangle further on the issue, for his other close family members to be brought into the discussion, for him to be pressured into changing his mind. Cantankerous Bharwani, however, died suddenly the following day, bequeathing me such a predicament that it would seem as if I was caught inside a maze from which there was no exit.

Once a death reaches notice of the community organs, as somehow it does almost immediately, the funeral committee goes into high gear. Cemetery management is requested to prepare the next available site, the body is sent for ritual washing and embalming, the funeral date is set and announced; relatives in different cities in the world learn about the death within hours and arrange for services in their local mosques. This is the way it always is.

"What should I do," Yasmin said to me over the phone from the hospital. "They have taken over, and I don't know what to say to them. . . ."

If I had said, Nothing, she would surely have been relieved. It is what I felt strongly inclined to say—Do nothing, let them take over; he's dead anyhow, it won't make any difference to him. But it does make a difference to us, the living, how we dispose of the dead.

Does that sound right?

"What do you think you should do?" I probed her gently.

"My conscience tells me to follow his wishes, you know I promised I would. But I don't know what's right. I don't want him to go to hell or some such place because of his arrogance. Is there a hell, Mukhisaheb? What exactly do we believe in?"

She had me there. I had learned as a child that hell was the name of the condition in which the human soul could not find final rest in the Universal Soul; in that case the body was simply useless and disposable baggage. I was also told of a Judgment Day, when the body would be raised, and of a heaven where you had a lot of fun, presumably with many pretty young women, and in contrast a hell where you went to burn for your sins while giant scorpions gnawed at your guts. I was inclined toward the more sublime approach to the hereafter—though who has returned from the world of the dead to describe conditions there? It seemed a safe bet simply to follow tradition, to go with the blessings and prayers of your people. But mere tradition was not enough for Karim Bharwani; he liked to make up his own mind. He had never played it safe. How were we going to send him off, and into what?

I didn't answer her question. "Your husband has put us into a real quandary, Yasmin," I said instead. "Give me some time to think. Perhaps we can delay the funeral by a day, let me try and arrange that."

"His family has already started arriving, for the funeral . . . it's a big family . . . two brothers and two sisters and cousins and aunts and uncles, and his mother. What am I going to say to them?"

"Say nothing for now."

"I don't know what I would have done without you, you truly are a godsend."

Isn't that what I was supposed to be? But I found myself confounded, I didn't know what to do, where my duty lay.

I called up Jamal and Nanji, two other classmates from way back, to talk about "Communist" Bharwani's death, and we reminisced some. It was the first death to strike our group from school, not counting a tragedy in grade eleven, when a friend was hit by a truck. They told me that Alidina, Kassam, Samji, and perhaps a few others would also be arriving, from out of town, for the funeral. Bharwani was lucky, so many of his former classmates would be present to pay him their respects. Would he appreciate that? We believed so.

He was always intense, always controversial. Broad shouldered and not very tall, he had a habit of tilting his head leftward as he walked. He parted his thick black hair in the middle and, even more outrageous for the time (this was high school), wore suspenders to school. He spoke English with a twang that made people laugh, for its foreign imitation, until they heard what he was saying, which always seemed profound. He was our star debater and actor. One day he brought in a four-page indictment of God, obviously culled from books of literature, and presented the typescript to our hapless religion teacher, one Mr. Dinani, who broke into tears and called Bharwani "Lucifer," which thrilled him ever so much. Mr. Dinani lives in Scarborough now, an insurance salesman recently awarded a plaque by his company for record sales. I lost touch with Bharwani when he went to England for university. When I saw him years later in Toronto, he seemed distant and perhaps even a bit disdainful; I gathered that my vocation as a real estate agent and my role as community worker did not meet his standards of achievement.

That night there was the usual sympathy gathering of family and friends, after services in my mosque, where I met my former classmates, six in all. Yasmin sat in the midst of the large Bharwani clan, beside her mother-in-law, a severe-looking though diminutive woman with hennaed hair furiously and silently counting her beads. Mr. Dinani too was present, and in his familiar, overwrought manner, was already in tears. But my former friends and I gathered afterwards at Jamal's lavish house on Leslie Street and gave ourselves a great reunion party, at which we remembered old "Communist."

Alidina, a heart surgeon in Kingston, recalled how Bharwani used to read and edit his English compositions at school. Once a small guy, fondly nicknamed "Smidgin," Alidina was now simply broad and short, a recently divorced man turned out in an expensive suit. According to a rumour I'd heard, he had been accused by his wife, at a reconciliation hearing, of almost strangling her. His imitation of Bharwani's arrogant manner was predictably hilarious. Nanji gave us a story the rest of us had never heard before. Late one afternoon, after classes were long over, while he was walking along a corridor he had chanced upon Bharwani and the new chemistry teacher Mr. Sharma sitting together in a classroom at the teacher's table; Mr. Sharma was in tears and Bharwani was patting him on the hand to comfort him. What to make of that? Bharwani with a tender heart was not an image we were familiar with.

The stories wove on, recalled after many years, inevitably embellished; the evening wore on, a good portion of the people getting progressively drunk, sentimental, louder. At these moments I always find myself adrift in my soberness. I debated briefly with myself whether to let them in on Bharwani's last wish, but decided the moment was not quite the right one to request intelligent input from my friends. I left, taking my secret with me, though I could not help warning Jamal in somewhat mysterious fashion that I might need his legal advice on a serious matter. As I drove through Jamal's gate, the question of the funeral seemed ever more urgent. Time was short. Wouldn't it be better just to let things be, let the burial proceed? No one would be the wiser, but for Yasmin, Farida, and me.

Messages were waiting for me when I arrived home. In one, I had been confirmed to preside over the funeral ceremony, which according to another message had been postponed from the next day to the one following, as I had requested. There was a frantic appeal from Yasmin—Please call, any time.

"I met with my in-laws today, to discuss procedures for the funeral ceremony," she told me when I called.

"Did you tell them of Karim's wish?"

"I didn't know what to say. I was waiting for your advice."

"What do your children think?"

"I've told all three of them. The older ones want to meet with you."

We agreed that I should go to meet her and the children early the next morning at her house.

The house is in an area of north Toronto called Glencedar Park, a locale so devoid of coloured faces— except for the nannies pushing strollers—as to appear foreign to the likes of me. A cul-de-sac, with access to it limited by one-way streets, the neighbourhood might remind the cynical minded of a fortress. There are not many such neighbourhoods left. I have taken clients to inspect houses in Glencedar Park, who after a single drive through it have instructed me simply to hasten out to somewhere else. Having parked my car and come out on the sidewalk, I met the curious though not unfriendly eyes of a couple of heads of households in long coats, each with a briefcase in hand and a folded paper under an arm, striding off to catch the subway on Yonge Street. I told myself this is where Bharwani had come to seek refuge from his people.

"How do you like the area?" I asked Yasmin when she opened the door.

"Very much," she said. "We've had no problems. Some of the neighbours are rather nice. The others keep to themselves."

All three children were waiting for me in the living room. The oldest, Emil, was a broad, strapping young man, conspicuously crowned with a crop of thick black hair slicked and parted in the middle, which reminded me of his father in his youth. He was at university. The second, Zuleikha, with the slim and toned looks of her age, resembled neither parent; she was finishing high school. The third child, Iqbal, was nine and rather delicate looking. They stood up and I went and embraced each in turn. I reminded myself that this was their time of sorrow, they had lost a father, who to me was only Bharwani, from a shared past, calling upon which he had put me in a delicate spot.

I muttered some inanities in praise of their father, my arm around the shoulders of little Iqbal, beside whom I had sat down, when Emil, after a nod from his sister, went straight to the point. "Mukhisaheb," he said, "our mother has told us about Dad's desire to be cremated. We would like to know what you think."

"Your father expressed that wish to me and your mother. I believe the ultimate decision is the family's."

"I think cremation's the best way," Zuleikha spoke up, sounding frivolously like an ad, which wasn't her intent. She had evidently not had much sleep, and she had spent time crying. There was a mild look of defiance in the glare she then awarded me. I have come to believe, in the few years I've held communal office, that to the young people I am a little like a cop, whom they would like to come to for help but whom they also resent.

"I differ," Emil said stiffly. "But of course Dad's wishes matter."

"I don't want Dad to be burnt," broke the quivering voice of young Iqbal beside me, and I held him tight at the shoulders as he gave a sob. His mother, saying to him, "Come," took him from me and out of the room.

This is a close family, I observed to myself. I thought of my own son, who had left home soon after graduating from school and was now in Calgary, never quite having looked back; and of my daughter, the same age as Zuleikha, who had grown distant from Farida and me.

"The problem is," I told Emil and Zuleikha, "that cremating is not in our tradition—you know that. It might even be forbidden on theological grounds. The community will not allow it. And there are other family members—your father's mother, and his brothers and sisters. They will have something to say, too."

"But he was *our* father, we have the right to decide," the girl said emphatically.

"What can the community do?" asked her brother.

"They can refuse the final rites to the body," I told him.

"Does that matter?" asked Zuleikha. "It wouldn't have mattered to Daddy. He would have refused them anyway, if he could."

"Your mother wishes the final rites and prayers."

Their mother brought in fresh brewed coffee and a plate of cookies. "He'll be all right," she told me, with a smile, referring to Iqbal. "I'm trying to explain to him that his father lives on in spirit." She quickly averted her eyes, so expressive of the turmoil and grief beneath her surface. In a cream cardigan over a dark green dress, she reminded me of how young women used to dress back in Dar a long time ago, during the cooler hours of the day. She had been trained as a librarian, as I was aware, and now worked in government. Ever since her call to tell me that her husband had closed his eyes for the last time while in the midst of chatting with her and Iqbal, she seemed to have kept her emotion in check.

Emil said: "Mum, what would *you* like to do, regarding Dad?"

"It sounds silly, I know, but I only want to do what is right."

"What is right is what *he* wanted," her daughter insisted, and tossed another glare at me. I could imagine her as Daddy's favourite, always ready at his defence during conflicts.

"Let's all give it a few more hours," I told them. "The funeral is tomorrow. Meanwhile . . . if you wish, you could inquire about cremation procedures and costs. . . ."

By that evening the community leadership had caught wind of Bharwani's last wish, and I received a stream of phone calls, all intended to sound me out regarding rumours already in circulation. No, I was certain, I replied, that the family was not considering alternative funeral arrangements. The ceremony would take place tomorrow, as announced. And, yes, I had seen Karim in hospital, delivered chhanta to him, he had not been out of his mind, ranting ignorant things. Finally came the call from the very top, the chummy but very commanding voice of our Chairman. "What is there to these rumours, Shamshu— something about the deceased's wish to be cremated. Word is that he spoke to you before he died, and that you are close to his family." I explained to him what the situation was and told him that since I was a witness to that last wish of the dead man, I felt somewhat obligated by it. The last remark was wilfully ambiguous, and I waited for his response. "We understand your personal predicament, Shamshu," the Chairman answered impatiently, "but first and foremost you are a mukhi; not just a presider but a representative of God. You know what is right. Just because the deceased had deviated from the right path— that's what I hear, he had become a communist—does that mean it is not our duty to try and save him? And it seems to me that this is the perfect opportunity, when he has fallen back into our hands. You said he let you do chhanta; that means he had a semblance of faith still left in him. Then let's save him. Otherwise he dies without the prayers of his people to go with him."

His was the kind of pompous, authoritarian voice that prompts one to rebel. What did the man know of the right path except that it was the official path, I caught myself asking, echoing Bharwani perhaps.

"It's his wife's and children's desire to fulfill his wish," I said.

"Then obviously they are misled. You can convince them as to what is right, can't you? If not, I'll give them a call myself."

He didn't wait, though, for twenty minutes later, while I prevaricated and sounded out Farida on what to do, Yasmin called.

"Mukhisaheb, the Chairman himself called. There doesn't seem much choice now. . . ." Her voice petered out.

All she wanted was to be told what was right. The Chairman had done that, but she wanted to hear it from me. At that moment I made up my mind.

"Listen, Yasmin," I told her. "You and the children should decide for yourself. I can't advise you what to do. But the funeral ceremony will happen tomorrow. It's up to you and your children whether you choose to bury or cremate their father."

She took a long moment before saying, "All right."

Emil called that evening, and we talked for a while. Then Zuleikha called and said, "Thank you, Mukhisaheb. I know my father was right to depend on you." She added, just before hanging up: "You know what? Some of my uncles have found out about this, and may try to stop us. But we are ready. The law is on our side, isn't it?"

"I believe so," I answered, having checked with my legal expert Jamal in the meantime.

"If your conscience wills it that way," was Farida's response to my decision. Bharwani's desire to be cremated had appalled her, actually; she saw it as mischievous and divisive. But she, if anyone, knew that my resolution had not been an easy one to arrive at; and we both were too aware that the final outcome tomorrow was far from certain, and repercussions in the days ahead would yet have to be faced.

Laid out before me and my associate performing the funeral rites, Bharwani looked a meagre, helpless rendition of his old self in the funeral casket. In small groups selected members of the congregation came and knelt before him, on his other side, and went through the ritual in which the dead is forgiven of sins. Earlier on I had spotted Iqbal and gone to give him a comforting pat on the shoulder. I had developed a possessive, protective instinct for him. We stood together, and when I went to take my place for the ceremonies he came and sat down beside me on the carpet, watching people come and kneel before his dead father.

Yasmin was wearing a white shalwar kameez, a dupatta covering her head—a mode of dressing that was never traditionally ours but, ironically, has been recently acquired in Canada. Beside her sat her mother-in-law pulling at her beads frantically, her head lowered, and the sisters-in-law. Bharwani's two brothers and other male relations sat grimly in a large group directly in front of me, ready for battle; somewhat to the side and quite distinct from them sat Emil with a few young men. It took me a while to find Zuleikha, also sitting away from her family.

The ceremony over, I stood up, motioning for the casket to be left as it was, and made a short speech. I said that our brother Karim Bharwani had made his wish known at his death bed that he wanted to be cremated. Karim, who was a classmate of mine, was a deep-thinking and not frivolous man. I had been told that his wife and children wished to respect our dead brother's last wish. Whatever our own beliefs were, we should open our hearts and respect their decision.

I motioned to the funeral committee to pick up the coffin and begin the chant, so that the male family members and congregation could carry it away. The women of the family began to weep.

"We do not cremate our dead, it is a sin!" boomed a deep voice from the back of the hall. It was the Chairman.

For moments nothing moved, there came only the moaning, sobbing sounds of the women. I was the person officially in charge, and the weight of all stares was upon me. I nodded to Emil, whereupon he and two hefty friends stepped forward to lift the casket. They gathered at the front end, somewhat nervously awaiting reinforcements, when promptly the dead man's brothers and a third man came and took hold of the back. The coffin was raised—and there ensued a tug-of-war.

At first, equal forces applied from the front and the back, the coffin hung still. Then it lurched forward, where the greater strength of the younger men lay. But these boys relaxed their hold and a sudden pull came from behind, where two large women had now joined forces. A fair crowd had gathered and was pulling aggressively at the back, having sensed victory for that side, ready to hand it charge—but two or three of those at the very back tripped and fell, bringing their end of the coffin with them. Poor Bharwani, after being buffeted this way and that in his box, was brought to rest at a forty-five-degree angle.

There was stunned silence, and then the eerily thin quivering sound of a snicker that turned heads. It was Yasmin, caught in a hysterical fit. Tears streamed down her face as she laughed, Zuleikha holding on to her shoulders. The women around them had moved away in fear.

In disgust I turned to Bharwani's relations: "Is this what you wish for him, this circus? To what holy end?"

Shamefaced, they retreated from the coffin, which was brought back to rest on the floor. Then Jamal, Nanji, and the rest of the classmates at one end, and Emil and two pals in front, unescorted by anyone else, the coffin bearing Bharwani slowly made its way to the door, outside which two hearses awaited to carry the dead to either of the two arrangements which had been made for him.

Bharwani, you won, I muttered, as I closed the door of my car on Iqbal, who was accompanying me to the crematorium. There were four cars in the procession that left the mosque, far fewer than would normally have accompanied the cortège, and our escorting policemen sped us through the traffic in no time.

My new friend Iqbal was chatty in the car. "When a person dies, he leaves the body, isn't that so? So the body is just flesh, and even begins to smell and rot."

I nodded. "Yes. That's why we have to bury it or . . . cremate it, as soon as possible." Or leave it exposed for vultures to eat, I said to myself.

"My dad is alive somewhere, I know."

"I know that too."

Is It Still October

*Is it still October, he asks, turn-*ing around wide-eyed and apprehensive, as if the month passed while he was trying to sleep.

Yes, my dear, it's still October, I say to him in the dark.

And so it will remain for you, always, and for me; and many of your friends will not see much of the new month either.

What a bore, this Halloween that's now over. And it's

not because I wasn't born here, didn't have *trick-or-treat!* as a kid: where is the *passion* in this festival, I ask you? It's all mechanical, merely *duty*. Six p.m., the toddlers are the first to arrive at the door, the cute angels pushed forward by an anxious parent; seven, the pirates and witches come, and at eight a few teenage louts in garish rubber masks, with pounding footsteps and heavy breathless voices, loaded with garbage bags containing candies. Six in the morning the next day, tomorrow, the pumpkin chucked out in the garbage. Business as usual, all's forgotten, and on to another theme, in this ongoing conspiracy between shopkeepers who'll sell a condom to your grandfather and teachers devoted to work-free "theme" days. And the *tons* of candies in this tight-assed Frigidaire of a community best characterized by a certain insect with a sting. A clear half of the sweets is dumped out with the pumpkin, at least in this household. That's dollars and cents sacrificed in the name of neighbourhood relations, much good that's done. And what do those tooth-sharpeners the dentists say about this candy madness?—nothing, simply rub their hands in glee, seeing the down payment on the Jag or that Cessna. . . . *Who wants gum?—I do, I do.* . . .

Ouch, the tooth hurts, but damn if I'll go to one of those rapacious drillers—not now, anyway. Live with the pain, die with the pain.

Poisons and painkillers. A poison is a painkiller, ultimate. And the weapon of a thinker, a schemer, as opposed to a gun. Like chess is to football. Like a certain nitrosamine compound. Tasteless, odourless, with cousins abiding safely in your homely and much maligned spinach; or adding zap to jet fuel. The wonders of chemistry. (The wonders of poison.) Replace one radical in your vegetable extract with another and you make yourself a first-class killer, cooler than a Beretta. Satanic, spreadable. Have death, will travel. That's all it takes to make a killer—a small change, an emendation. Inject a smidgin in the bloodstream and all the elaborate machinery of evolution, this pinnacle of organized matter, this genius of chemistry and electric impulses, comes to naught. Unrevivable. Biodegradable. Slime into dust, worms into flesh. Fertilizer. But suppose this elaborate circuitry, these electric impulses, can be revived, memory and all? Then God will not exist, for there will be no one to answer to. And killing will have to be more thorough. But that's too far away, today and tomorrow bodies will decompose.

In my mind's eye I hear a scream; if I let this mind tarry, then a blood-curdling scream, yes. I feel grief, a bit, a residue, deep somewhere—who wouldn't?—but most of me stays cold. Because I have crossed over, to the evil, the satanic; the painless. I know there is no good or evil. There is only possibility and experience, there is curiosity and numbness; bitterness, anger, calmness, vindication; and bemusement, we all have to face death, it comes unannounced, knows no night or day, child or adult, coldly plucks out its appointed victim—isn't that what we were always told? And—if you ever believed it—we all live out our appointed share of life. I never did believe that, even as a child in a religious household. But this much I know, to the dying, death comes without notice. And this case, at least, *this* present case evolving even now as I think these thoughts sitting on the floor beside my angel's bed, will be without violation of the purity of innocents, will be truly nonviolent in the most important way.

There are two kinds of poison—those that strike the nervous system, and those the circulatory system. So said my first snake book. *Snakes? Ur-rurr!* Who would want to study snakes, the devil's own creation, cold-blooded terror slithering silently underfoot . . . well, what's wrong with finding out? Most snakes are, well, nonviolent, and those who can will hurt you when frightened. I got interested in them because of what I'd heard. The chhatu—python—so big and powerful, just by opening its mouth and drawing breath it could pull in and ingest a dog at, say, twenty feet. And the cobra, my mother would say, the black naag who if you kill its mate will follow you to the end of the earth and seek revenge in your veins—and so the fate of a man who had been followed by a she-cobra all the way from India to Africa, over the black waters. A story to make you shudder and dream in terror afterwards. And then of course, still talking snakes and poisons, Elizabeth Taylor—Cleopatra—and the viper, oh what tenderness toward a snake, what dignity to death. And Eve and the serpent. On thy belly shalt thou crawl, but the snake had the last laugh, spine-shaped, hairlike, penislike, smiling its toothless smile that sends shudders down the . . . well, spine.

But mother didn't talk about scorpions—except how one got into one of her cousin's ears. Nothing about how the female stings and kills its mate after mating. . . . Does the male scorpion actually find the female beautiful?

How tenderly beautiful did my little arachnid look, once upon a wedding night in Karachi, delicate and fragile, her face pink and rouged, lips red and full, puckered Madhuri-like, white sari sequinned, the end going over the black hair. *O piece of the moon*, my heart sang, she was full and ripe, ready to be plucked—*fucked*—and I did just that. I drew blood. Only, she took two decades and four kids before she stung back, this pro-lifer, drew all the money from our accounts and fled with Pious Ayub. And left me with this freak. Nature's chromosomically slight deviation from the template labelled "normal."

Freak, but how tender and human, how loving he can be . . . when those fragile arms go around the neck and he clings, and how sensitive to hurt, and what a laugh and mischief, what embodiment of life. As if sensing I was the one who would have terminated his gestation, he's reserved his devotion for me. And his mother, who had insisted on having him, finally abandoned him to me and absconded.

Yes, it's still October, my angel, but just. . . . How you tug at my heart, how I wish you had had a semblance even of normalcy in your life—a reasonably happy home, McDonald's and Gerrard Street and Wonderland, Centre Island, monopoly and cards, and baseball, and holidays out of town. But for you it was wrong from the word go; and you yourself didn't add up.

Child, child. . . .

The last of the teenage louts stomp away from the front door disappointed, dragging their sacks full of goodies. The jack-o'-lantern on the porch has flickered out. A fat but not full moon slides through wispy clouds this cold night. The last of the maple leaves hang limply from their trees. The quiet houses of this lovely, traditional street exude cosy warmth through their windows.

Yes, a beautiful street of old English-style red-brick houses with sloping roofs and bay windows, hung over with grizzled maples. As in the storybooks; you should see it after a snowfall. *She* would have preferred *new!-new!-new!* and far-away, closer to the North Pole, a dream mansion in a brand-new development, with houses six deep and saplings planted on the sidewalks hopefully to give shade in two decades, by which time the area would be overrun by neo-Nazis, Jamaican warlords, and the Russian mafia. She didn't object past the first demurral—there's status to living in an all-white neighbourhood, provided you don't let on about the unnerving experiences. Those little slights that are almost not there; but they are. Soon after we moved in, as we unloaded groceries in the driveway, a guy walked past saying, How did *you* find yourselves here? Same way as you, sucker, I shouted back, we're here and we're taking over. Fat chance, I wish I'd had the presence of mind to say just that. Meanwhile our three were the only brown kids in school, besides one black and one half-Japanese. Try that for comfort. Try telling the kids they're not white, not better than black nor worse than anyone else. And the neighbours, a reserved kind, the stiff-upper-lip sort—at least as far as we're concerned; because when a white couple moved in three months after us, the whole street came up to shake hands with them and kiss their blue-eyed angels, these Ontarian patriots come to defend the Anglo fort. But so what? These enclaves have to be broken in, neutralized, *multiculturalized.* That argument is similar to the one I used for bringing into our home a Christmas tree: let's make the tree *ours!* She wouldn't have it. But what do we have that's so festive? I demanded. We have Eid, but what fun is it anymore? Christmas is in the *air* we breathe, as once Eid and Diwali were. Let's move then, she insisted, to somewhere where we have people and can celebrate our festivities. No. No, no, no! Give satisfaction to these stuck-up prigs, these escapees from 1776, and freedom, these British-but-Americans? Give satisfaction to *him,* the single-handed destroyer of my career? . . . upon whom, however, the angel of death is moving in, as he did against the Egyptians. . . .

Hi, Jim, I said, having plucked up courage, running into him outside Loblaws, next to the bank machine and the Chinese flower shop. On his arm a ravishing young woman . . . long blonde hair, stylish winter jacket, tight jeans. (Wild, roving eye I still have, can't help that.) Looked like his daughter. He, too, in dashing ski jacket, red and grey. They towered over me, both of them—and hurried straight past. He without even a flicker of a greeting, though she sized me up for an instant, must have asked him about me later. On my lips, my unspoken greeting, frozen: Guess we're neighbours now! That snub hurt so badly. Why did I have to bother, but then what do you do when you run into a guy from the Department whom you see every day at work. Someone with influence. A few minutes later they returned (I was still at the bank machine) followed by an assistant carrying a Christmas tree. They had it put in the back of their Volvo station wagon and drove off.

Jim Burton, the man who shot down my ambition early in my career, now spurning me in the street, brushing off my existence as if I were some kind of street Arab (isn't that the expression?) when I made that first gesture at some kind of new beginning between us. We're neighbours now. I moved into his area, though on a modest street, in a modest house. Perhaps he didn't see me, saw someone else. How could *I* have moved into his area? Through painstaking work and scrounging, that's how. By grinning and bearing it at work, playing the Indian Sambo.

But twenty years ago . . . I still had a dream. And I will never forget that scene when, naive, scared, defenceless, I got crushed underfoot like a miserable cockroach—

Your project is good, excellent in fact, and your grades are remarkably good, considering you did your undergraduate studies in . . . er . . . somewhere else. Mysore, India, I put in. Ah, that explains that— Notwithstanding all that, your speech and manner of presentation . . . does not justify granting of a doctorate . . . not yet . . . don't you agree. . . . Looks around at his committee of cronies. What do you expect, of course they agree. Sorry and all that.

Anyone else would have granted me my Ph.D., but this nigger in the woodpile, this fly in the ointment, this pain in the ass—tall and dashing, Viking-like, the well-mannered senior professor whom I had venerated—turned them all against me. Manner of presentation—accent, you mean. Foreignness. Brown. Indian. Granting me a doctorate and allowing a brown face among their bleached selves, that's what put a chili up their ass. But, said our Viking, offering a sop, a master's with honourable mention, that you surely deserve. And we can offer you a job, with your expertise, that of a technician. Read: slave. A dead-end job as a white-coated jack-of-all-trades technician, non-union errand boy, reserved for all those desperate and too-timid immigrants from the East.

With your expertise. . . . I could teach them a thing or two, and he knew it. That's why he kept me on to do his experiments, and for twenty years I remained at his beck and call, the invisible hand behind his published successes. Well, Jim. Dr. Burton, watch out for a taste—a *tastelessness!*—of my next experiment!

The effects of toxins on babies is, of course, my specialty. Mouse babies only, so far. And dispatching them after the experiments. If I'd had my way I'd have dispatched this child too, now desperately trying to go to sleep on this Halloween night . . . though once he was born the two of us became thick as thieves, as close as can be, and there was nothing I wouldn't do for this tender soul whose Xs and Ys don't match up.

An X from the mum and a Y from the dad; that's how you make a boy. That's the instruction baby factories of the future will carry in their foremen's manuals, under MALE BABIES. One X or Y too many or too few and you have a deviant and the choice to abort. In our case, there was one X too many. A 47 baby boy. Midnight's child. What does this mean, doctor? There is a good chance that your child's sexual organs will not fully develop. For example. . . . Like, how? The testes may not develop and the ability to procreate—well, he will never be a biological father. But he'll be a boy—male? Yes . . . the stature will be smallish, but in most cases he will be a normal child—there's a lot you can do with postnatal—that's after-birth—therapies. And—to abort? The choice to abort is entirely yours (you can tell where her sympathies lie, and she eyes the mother, gauging reaction)—if you want, I can refer you to the terminations department. What kind of postnatal treatment—I press on—can the child be normal? For the first few years there will be regular consultation with physicians and surgeons . . . and as for normal, it all depends on what you mean by normal. But *what exactly* can go wrong, what are the statistics? I'm afraid the statistics are only now being compiled, and we don't have enough—the condition has only recently been understood, with more and more genetic testing before birth. (You mean in the past people accepted the babies they got and blamed deformations on God—and laughed at the freaks and teased them no end and gave them nicknames.) What else . . . can go wrong with the baby? the mother asks, for the first time. A look in the eye of the doctor, a call for a straight answer, to wit: Such conditions tend not to live beyond eighteen or so. But of course—

You're an expert at removing babies from their mothers' wombs, aren't you—she taunted, referring to my experiments on mice embryos under supervision of mein führer Jim Burton.

What was there to say? We accepted the child that God had decided to give us.

What God? The wife looked at me in horror when I uttered this blasphemy. From then on it was downhill all the way for the two of us. But the little boy became mine, and she lost interest in him.

Now she's gone off with Pious Ayub, having cleaned out all our savings, and I sit here on Halloween night keeping watch over my beautiful little monster. My jigger—liver as they used to say, my heart, my khoon, my blood, my soul, my everything. You know I love you. But I've reached my end, and without me you're nothing.

I remember Shanta Behn so clearly, every day these past few days she's grown clearer in my mind . . . the pale white face and long pigtail reaching down to her waist . . . now that I think of it she would have been in her twenties. The flip-flop slippers and the saris, thin but wide at the hips . . . does a sexual image form?—hard to say, but she must have been attractive and deeply unhappy, every day she'd come to the shop to buy groceries and Dad, he must have eyed her and picked his crotch as he was wont to do, absentmindedly as it were—Mum was wide-hipped too but fat, a waddling shrew. But one day Shanta Behn tied her two daughters to her waist with a length of sisal rope and set herself aflame. And I never forgot Shanta Behn, right up to that wart over the cheekbone, and those large, deep kohl-black eyes and yes, a faint odour of spices. . . .

But *you* will not go alone, my son, you will not go unnoticed. You will exit with fanfare, you will make a noise. Even now I hear their screams, I hear my old nemesis Jim howling somewhere in the night, I hear an ambulance. . . .

Work, poison, work. Like Asrael, mark out the Egyptians' homes and punish them. For their haughty arrogance and their hoity-toity racism. Work, poison, and lay out their pink babies in a row of death, like so many toxified mouse embryos.

After all, how many people can actually go beyond hopelessness or uncontrollable rhetoric or frustration and actually *achieve* vengeance—cold and exact retribution, risking all. Not just failure, arrest by those gun-toting wide-belted protectors of the white and rich; but risking all eternity, like Azazel. (What was Azazel before he defied, risked all? A nonentity, fairy. Now he's the equal of that vain Braggart.) It's only when you risk all that a shudder runs down your spine, your hair stands on end: you are alone and there is no God; no heaven and no hell. Rules are made by the powerful who demand you play by them. Reality is the world they have created, laws are what keep you from changing the rules. So it was in the time of the pharaohs; and so it is now. Except for those who strike out where they can. *I'll show you!* Yes, you have to *show* them. Else you become like one of those cartoon-caricature television Indo-Pakistanis. . . .

Irony is not wanting in my little drama, this playlet that will unfold into tragedy, so that perhaps the American president, the UN Secretary-General, and Nelson Mandela or Archbishop Tutu might feel compelled to issue statements of sympathy. The irony is that the ruin that is about to fall upon the House of Burton will have issued via the agency of the man he ruined and humiliated using the chemical agent he's world famous for, which he's used to destroy (through the agency of that same ruined, humbled man) hundreds of frightened mice and more than a thousand wriggling pink fetuses, all in order to trace the path of an amine poison in an organism (and to write dozens of technical papers and win a membership in the Royal Society). What perfect geometry, what fearful symmetry in this vengeance—it has to succeed if only because of this. Nature loves simplicity—A. Einstein.

And nature seeks its own agents to execute its precise plans? The future is preordained; events lead one from the other, logically, easily—as the winds move, the moisture gathers, the rain falls—and destroys a village. And the earth goes merrily along, the seasons change, *to every thing turn. . . .*

The perfect geometry existed, unrevealed. Dr. Burton gets another hefty grant from his peers, requests me to start work with that most potent of poisons, a nitrosamine, which had been my subject of study, a decade and a half ago when I still had a dream. The poison is kept on the top shelf of an overhead cabinet secured with a—guess what?—padlock! Not only can a padlock be cut with pliers, the latch to which it is attached can simply be broken by a twist of the padlock, or—you'll never believe this—*unscrewed!* Not only that, I have a *key* to the padlock. Talk of fate, talk of temptation, talk of revenge!

Come Halloween, end of October, and the perfect sequence of events reveals itself, a diamond glowing in the dark. A diamond, recall, possesses perfect crystalline-clear symmetry.

And so toffee and chocolates, gum, gobstoppers, gummi bears, fruit drops, sour balls . . . and that new craze of designer yuppie children with pinchable cheeks and smooth hair and bright clothes and their perfect parents: the psychedolipops, also a favourite of that old Viking

Jim Burton and his two grandkids, Scottie (boy) and Campbell (girl), by that golden-haired, lanky lass (Jemima). All these candies get coated by that tasteless monster of a poison—and trick *and* treat.

But now I can hear an ambulance—or two—and something's bound to have happened. . . . O Asrael, you've done your rounds, now come and take these hands and let me end October here for this child. His eyes must watch me as I press down the pillow: that, after all, is my ultimate judgment . . . my hell . . . how frail and willingly he comes, how trustingly he subsides—oh, God.

And now the sour balls for this loser, a sweet and sour death.

No, Jim, I did not go through with it; at least not at your end. Evil does not have to be punished; and mercy, noticed.

Elvis, Raja

I.

> *Ah-one ah-two ah-body in the*
country jail . . .

That's how we always heard it, way back when, and scratched our heads, confused—what's "nix, nix"? and what kind of name is Shifty Henry, anyway? And "getting kicks"?

Seven young people in black pants and white T-shirts and slicked hair doing nifty things on a stage, with wooden chairs and a gymnastics crossbar and a horse, to the sound of "Jailhouse Rock." A black student with a white-painted face stands holding a whip over a white student with blackened face, who's bent over a chair, clutching the seat, and is evidently a girl. She undulates and gyrates her taut shapely body, mouthing silent cries of pain or ecstasy every time the tip of the riding crop reaches out and caresses her bottom. To the far right a character in gym shorts and undershirt continuously pummels a punching bag; another character in jeans and jacket, boots and cowboy hat, broodingly stalks the stage for something, oblivious of the others, as if belonging to yet another, superimposed tableau. "*Flaming Star*," Diamond mutters to himself, identifying the latter scene. Rusty always knew all the Elvis stuff, movies and songs, as I did once, only I chose to outgrow and forget them. I never quite forgot, did I; though Rusty seems to have thrived on Elvis.

A long time ago Diamond and Rusty had arrived, shy freshmen, one from Nairobi the other from Bombay, to study in New York. But the world was on fire and soon there they were in long hair and new jeans, screaming, "Off the pigs!" with all the other students protesting against the Vietnam War, and "Ho Ho Ho Chi Minh!" Yet back in his Elvis-postered room late in the evenings, there would be Rusty behind his desk completing his home-work, his idol's songs playing on the stereo. One night an angry student radical clad in boots stormed in—while Elvis sang about a Chicago ghetto—and vented rage on Rusty's precious record collection, flinging it down on the floor, stamping on the black vinyl discs like they were cockroaches until they cracked. Grief-stricken Rusty shed many tears, and the following days scoured the city for all those old LPs and EPs he had lost.

Was it okay to stop over here, Diamond asks himself. We were friends once. We learned the ropes here, in this country, together. He tasted my first root beer for me and assured me it was not alcoholic; I cooked for him weekends, sometimes, chicken à la king and Salisbury steak and sloppy joe from plastic packages that you had to put in boiling water for three minutes. A few weeks after they met, they vowed to each other to have white girlfriends. An embarrassing memory. Why not just American girls or even black girls, since we so ardently supported the Black Panthers? But we came from the colonies and white is what we had to have, once. After graduation they had separated, and then a few years ago he had run into Rusty on a downtown street in Toronto. It was a couple of days after Christmas and Rusty was in town for an MLA conference. They had exchanged addresses, phone numbers, then failed to follow up on their lukewarm promises. He could have asked Rusty to come over for a coffee or a drink, but it was a busy period, his in-laws were in town, Sue's parents. Also, Diamond had felt a bit embarrassed: here was Rusty, a *professor*, and he, Diamond, an antique bookseller (a trade he learned from Sue's father) barely managing. Finally, when his old life crumpled up and disappeared into ashes, and he closed shop, when he was ready to hit the road to try something new, while poring over the maps, he told himself, I'll be passing by Rusty Mehta's college town, I could just drop in on him—for old times' sake. Not a bad idea to look up old friends and acquaintances at this stage in one's life.

Three hours out of Chicago he took the exit for Greenfield, checked in at a Howard Johnson just outside of the town, and called up Rusty at his college. That was yesterday afternoon. They had set up an appointment. "I have something to show you," Rusty said. And, weirdly, said his so-long with "Elvis lives! Jai Elvis!"

And now on the stage, in front of a class of twenty-five students and six visitors, stands Rusty Mehta. A little thicker at the waist than before, the hair short and bristly and gleaming black, a trimmed black goatee and moustache, the thick devil's eyebrows that always gave him an intense, insectile look, enhanced today by the black poloneck jersey, pants, and platform shoes. Perhaps it is that somewhat freaky face and the jeers it received in a Bombay convent school that drove him to withdraw into his Elvis religion.

"Today's performance is specially requested by our guests sitting at the back—they are local and known to us, most of them, though one visits us all the way from Toronto, an old friend. Welcome all. We are happy to oblige, and I say this on behalf of everyone involved. The cabaret you've seen," he tells the guests, "is to be presented at the Emerging Cultures Conference in December—to illustrate a paper on Elvis first as agent then as icon of subversion, from 'JH Rock' to the present. Also to entertain, of course," he smiles, pauses for effect, and is rewarded with restrained but knowing laughter from his students.

He still is, in fact now he truly is, a radical, Diamond thinks, squirming in his wooden auditorium seat, and he is utterly crazy, of course. It's not always wise to visit the past, I should have known that, but the point now is, I am here and how should I extricate myself gracefully from this entanglement.

"What you have seen," Rusty the insectile professor tells his audience, as the props are discreetly dismantled and carried away by the student players behind him, "is a musical memorial to a revolution. Elvis was a revolutionary as surely as Che was, or Ginsberg, or Malcolm X. And 'Jailhouse Rock' was subversion, it closed the coffin and danced to the demise of the stiff, sanitized world of *My Three Sons, Father Knows Best,* and Bing Crosby—the 'squares.' Some people—misguided boomers—believe the Beatles and Rolling Stones began the revolution, but if you look at how they began—just think of 'A Hard Day's Night'—you'll realize that Elvis was years ahead— Elvis was revolution in the raw and with the force of an express train."

Wasn't there an Indian Elvis once, a Bombay product, in the sixties? Some Singh or the other who sang, "Oh-oh-oh meri bebi doll?"

"Right," says Rusty, and Diamond thinks, we probably had this conversation decades ago. They are walking toward lunch at the Student Union cafeteria, with the five others from today's audience, who are in the lead and in passionate dialogue. Diamond tries to pick up the pace, in a bid to join them, but what's this—Rusty pulls him back by the arm.

"For me, Elvis never died," he says in quiet monotone.

Diamond grins. "I can see that."

"I'm one of the pioneers in Elvis Studies in this country. It wasn't easy to get my course accepted, I can tell you that. I teach Elvis as protest. His early movies, especially, had the real protest stuff—against poverty, racism, and colonialism—but he got hijacked, first by the government and the army, and then by showbiz. There is even the possibility of . . . the c-word . . . one dare not say it—" He looks Diamond squarely in the eye, then says it: "Conspiracy. Think of Kennedy—who also stood for the less privileged and the blacks—"

"In this case?—I mean, Elvis?"

"They neutered him—or tried to, but didn't succeed. If you study some of his later songs, you'll find the same message as before—sympathy for the poor and oppressed. He had to be careful not to overdo it . . . but in his movies, under the guise of dance and song he could be freer and you see a *multicultural* Elvis—" Rusty eyeballs Diamond keenly, as if to gauge his trustworthiness. "Yes, the m-word—gives some of these fellows here the creeps. Elvis preached it. He *was* it—he had black, Jewish, and Native Indian blood in him, though you won't read that in many places. And let me tell you this—even in death, *more so in death*, Elvis is a force to reckon with—"

"Come again? Why more so in death?"

The others have stopped to watch them, and Rusty adds hurriedly, "I can talk to you about it later, if you're interested," and they catch up with the rest.

They combine two tables in the cafeteria, bring their soups and sandwiches from the self-serve counter, and once settled, Rusty Mehta is allowed—not without knowing glances passed among his colleagues—to hold forth, if only for the benefit of his friend from Toronto.

"I was on CNN once," Rusty says, slurping his soup. "Did you see me?—I guess not." He is in a hurry and

Diamond suspects the discourse is not only for his benefit but also for the others, who have allowed themselves
to be captive for once.

Rusty says, "And I told CNN exactly what I thought
is the message of Elvis. I told them I believed Elvis had
Jewish and Native Indian *and* African ancestry. That's
when I got the Klan on my back."

"Really?" Diamond exclaims. Men wearing sheets, on
horseback; flaming crosses. Guns. Lynchings. "*Really?*"

"Yes. The Klan is very much alive and well in
Greenfield, Illinois, I'm happy to report."

"Oh come now Rusty, it's only a fringe group," protests
Phillip, a colleague, wearily called upon to defend the
local reputation once again. "The town was treated to a
procession of this so-called KKK—six guys in hoods—a
bunch of kooks who were booed from beginning to end."

"Yes, Rusty, a bunch of yahoos, no one takes them
seriously, you know that."

That's Janet; she twinkles a pleasant smile at Diamond
and explains, "I've got to say my bit too, we all like Rusty
but have to bring him back to earth, you understand. . . ."

She has an Ivory-soap plain face, observes Diamond.
We're all from the same generation. We could start a
"where were you when—" session, and sing familiar
songs for each other. No, I wasn't at Woodstock, wish I
had been, but I had to work summers to pay tuition.

"You may think that's a joke," Rusty says, "but when I
see guys in hoods with a raised cross outside my house,
I get scared."

"But you told us before they don't actually *burn* the
cross," says Phillip. "That doesn't make them Klan."

"Well, they wear those white sheets and make a disturbance outside my house late in the evening, and that scares my family."

The discussion continues. Diamond, at the farther end from Rusty, detaches himself from it, so does Janet. "I was in Seattle," she says, speaking of 1970, which came up a minute ago. "Lots of action there, that spring. Remember, the Vietnam protests? Kent State in the spring? I guess it was all a bit silly, really. I guess it didn't mean much to you, as a foreigner...."

"Foreign is where the war was," he says and smiles. She takes note.

Sure, we did our bit in the sixties, Rusty and I. Free Bobby Seale and all that. And we were right there, cheering outside, while the university president's office was occupied, we helped to burn draft cards outside the ROTC building, the two of us foreigners. Nerves tingling and heart racing as the National Guard chases you ... and later, Sue's father raising a finger, cautioning against extremism.

She reminds me rather of my Susan, he thinks, watching Janet return from the counter with her coffee. She has on a brown skirt, beige shirt, and blue denim vest—quite pretty with that absent, withdrawn look; and that blond hair must have been long and silky once, in 1970. But she doesn't look like Sue, who had thick, black, wavy hair. You would prefer me to have long and silky blond hair falling down my back wouldn't you, Sue had said a couple of times, and he told her, No, that's not true, black and wavy is more like Indian and better. That wasn't quite accurate, or honest. But we loved each other.

He met her at a used-book store on Broadway that he frequented. She used to help out there sometimes, the store belonged to her father. There would be flyers on the counter and he always made it a point to pick up a few. They were about strikes and protests, music recitals, lectures, and spiritual enlightenment. He happened to discuss an upcoming Ravi Shankar concert with the girl at the counter, and they wound up going to it together. That's how it started.

"Do you have a family in Toronto?" Janet asks.

"Are you married?—is the question—" someone quips.

"And it is nobody's business," says Phillip. Tall, with curly Art Garfunkel hair, smiling pleasantly.

"I was," Diamond speaks up. "She died."

There is a guilty silence.

"Sorry . . . ," Janet says. Then: "Was she sick?"

He nods.

"I say, Diamond," Rusty says, "you've got to check out of that motel and stay at my place. There's room enough and there are lots of things I have to show you, there are things to discuss."

"You bet!" comes a snide remark.

"I have to hit the road early tomorrow," Diamond replies across the table. "It would be more convenient where I am, I think."

"Let's talk about it later."

They leave noisily, reminding each other of the party at Rusty's place that night.

Was she sick? he often gets asked, and he always nods his reply. AIDS, he should add. No, I don't carry it myself.

She had a brief, thoughtless affair, that's how she caught it. How could she—the affair, the AIDS—after twenty years and more of marriage, a life together like this (fingers crossed together)? The inexplicable. The baby grand falling on your head as you walk by a tall apartment building. The impossible. She took a routine test at her doctor's, and he was asked to go with her to discuss the results. At the medical centre, where they'd known him the two decades he'd been in Toronto, they all stared at him: the women at reception, Nurse Cameron, and finally Dr. Berger. How could you, you louse: the looks on their faces. It wasn't I who infected her, he said patiently, and Sue nodded rapidly beside him. He could have caught it from her, only he hadn't. How could she. But then why not, when fifty's staring you in the face: and you ask yourself have I lived, really *lived*, before the decay begins—the heart, the arthritis, the prostate, the ovaries, as the case may be. When did the heart last throb in delicious, wicked excitement? Yes, there had been opportunities for him too, friendly female customers, over-forty types, an assistant once, a healthy-looking English major who liked his eccentricity, she said, his taste in books and music, and there was the backroom, enticing. But he had resisted, and not like Gibraltar either, he just didn't want the bother. Let's say I have lived and there's a life of the mind. And there's the commitment I have made. Perhaps he was plain chicken. But she, his Sue, had succumbed to wicked temptation.

　　—*I wronged you, Di. . . .*
　　—*Perhaps you did. I hope you didn't stop loving me.*
　　—*I didn't, honest, Di . . . all those years together.*

—Yes, all those years, they're ours.

My Peggy Sue, he'd sing to her when they were younger, during those special moments, after a quarrel, perhaps, and he'd be holding her, feeling terribly sorry; or when he'd woken up early some weekend morning and, leaning on his elbow, caressing the stray locks of her hair at the forehead, trying to wake her. There's no Peggy in my name, she would sometimes remind him gently. But it sounds nice with Sue, he'd tell her.

What could replace those moments?

Phillip plays the guitar, as does Janet beside him, in front of the fireplace in the living room. Janet moved out here after a divorce back east. Phillip is separated, his wife having left him to take up abode with a woman, taking the two kids with her. Which is fine by him. They sing Dylan and Joplin, and Simon and Garfunkel. How songs highlight an age—nothing, but nothing can detach them from us, however corny they sound to a later generation. In that they give us away. Elvis does not feature tonight; Elvis did not belong to their time, except for Rusty, and he had to do his worshipping in secret. Diamond requests "Tom Dooley," which he hasn't heard in ages, and is from way before the sixties, but they oblige; then he asks for "Charlie on the MTA," a Boston song which no one quite remembers. And so everyone is happy except Rusty, looking subdued and somewhat drunk.

Rusty's wife Vina is of such enchanting grace and angular beauty as to seem utterly and bizarrely alien in these surroundings. She has an ivory-white face, liquid black eyes, dark black hair, a thrilling, husky voice, and a lovely expression on her face. Her costume is Indian, a handworked silver long tunic over black pants. Cleopatra, Diamond thinks, unsettled by her attention to him, and gushes out compliments.

"Yes?" she says, staring back, her eyes melting him.

They have come to sit at the threshold, on the step down from the long passageway of the house into the sunken living room where the rest of the guests have spread out on sofas and the floor. Behind them is the dining room, its lights out. Both rooms face the front.

"Does Rusty know how fortunate he is, you are the most beautiful woman I've ever met."

Vina nods abstractedly and goes to check on the desserts and coffee, then returns to Diamond's side.

"Where did you learn to make such flattering comments?" she asks mischievously.

He is flattered that she heard him despite her preoccupations as the hostess.

"I assure you I don't normally talk like this," he says, realizing he is rather tipsy, but reassuring himself with drunken obstinacy, She *is* amazing, and so I'm doubly justified in making this asinine declaration.

"I understand you've been having a bit of trouble over the Elvis business," he tells her, hoping she will not leave him on the step by himself.

"Yes, our nocturnal visitors. They have not shown themselves for a few weeks, and we're hoping they've given up."

He decides not to pursue the disquieting subject and asks instead, "How did you meet Rusty?"

That takes her by surprise. Her face colours, but she recovers instantly. "Our meeting was arranged," she says, looking straight at him as if to challenge any adverse reaction or misunderstanding. "He came to Bombay from the States, looking for a bride. I had to approve him, of course. I quite liked him. I wanted to go to America like all young people—and he meant freedom and was quite exotic, you know. He was a real catch. He had just been a year here, in Greenfield."

In the living room the singing's stopped, someone is suggesting a game of personal fantasies.

"Here, here, I'll start—listen—my fantasy has in it a female garbage-truck driver, a blond Scandinavian type, not masculine-looking but with a little looseness of limb and a casual style—"

Diamond and Vina exchange a smile, but at this moment Rusty comes and sits down beside his wife, who pats him on the hand. "Feeling tired?"

"Just a little, but I don't want to spoil the fun...." They look at each other tenderly, and he asks, "What were you two going on about?"

"I was telling Diamond how we met, dear."

"Ah, yes. What would I have done if you hadn't come along?"

"Probably married that girl at the supermarket you had a crush on," she smiles.

He looks severely at her, takes her hand and says, "I don't think so, my darling."

They turn to stare at Diamond, and he smiles sheepishly. "Now there's a happy couple," he says.

But Vina draws out a long look of pity for him. "Rusty told me," she says. "About your wife—"

"Susan," Diamond says. "Rusty had met her, in fact.

Do you remember, Rusty? Mendelsohn's Rare Books?"

Rusty pauses a moment, then replies, "Oh yes, I recall . . . the one with the curly black hair. So you married that girl?"

"Yes I did. My first girlfriend."

"She had cancer?" Vina asks.

Diamond nods. "It's hard to believe when it's all over, but when it does happen, it's quick and sudden."

"I'm so sorry. And you're going to Las Vegas, of all places?"

Diamond gives a laugh. "Yes, of all places. Viva Las Vegas," he says and draws from Rusty a look of appreciation at this Elvis reference. "A family reunion. My brother's set himself up there, and the others are arriving all the way from Calgary and Vancouver, not to mention Toronto."

It's going to be emotional, this reunion, he hasn't seen Amir, his elder brother, for more years than he can remember. He never felt inclined to go to Las Vegas, and for Amir Toronto was beyond the beyond.

"Do you have any children?" she asks, and to his head shake, says wistfully, "We have only our Shireen. I couldn't have more."

Is it worth producing more children for the world? They used to ask each other, and answer firmly: No—there's enough misery in the world as it is. Instead of having children they would give to charities, adopt Third World children from a distance, help to make a better world. Actually they were both afraid of having children, and Sue was terrified because she had lost a younger sister in childhood. Twice to his knowledge she had woken up from a nightmare involving Marian.

Looking back now, would it have been worth having a child or two to call his own? He's been a good uncle, writing regularly to nieces and nephews, some of whom he's never met. In their discussions with one another, he's been told, they all think him odd but nice. One of them even described him as cool. "Give me a grandchild," Alfred Mendelsohn would tell his daughter, arguing, "producing heirs is a sacred duty, to God! To Humanity! Life is a gift, give it to someone. . . ." And Sue would reply with something like, "Dad, I'm not a factory for producing children"; or, "Dad, there are enough children in the world." Sue had a sister, Diane, who was also childless. There were no other siblings. Now Diamond wishes he and Sue had had children, and he'd have something that was both of theirs. Mendelsohn would have his grandchildren and heirs.

In the living room they are passing around joints. There is an embarrassed silence among the three of them on the step. Rusty refuses a joint with a shake of the head; snatches of "Love Me Tender" intrude, from a CD or tape. A table lamp, its ceramic middle shaped as Elvis, glows on an end table, the King's lips red and his slicked hair a dark purple.

People begin to take leave.

"Why don't you spend a day or two here?" Vina says to Diamond. "We would like that very much."

"That's what I've already asked him to do," says her husband. "We are like your family," he reiterates to Diamond. "Spend a couple of days with us. We can even go to the city and get a few Indian movies. And Vina's biryani is something you cannot pass over."

"Please do," she pleads, with those large black eyes that seem to see through his soul.

He says quickly, "Yes, I will, thank you. That's very nice of you. I'll go back tonight, and return tomorrow. How's that?"

And so it is agreed.

II.

The Mehtas' daughter Shireen opens the door, giving a warm smile. She is tall, thin, and pale, her oval face framed by jet-black hair tied behind in a loose ponytail. She has on an oversized yellow T-shirt over denims and has a cookie in her hand. An American child.

"Come in, Uncle," she says. "They're all in the den."

He puts his carryall down and she picks it up.

"Quality time, is it," he murmurs, and she giggles.

"Yes, as a matter of fact they're having tea."

And so into this Elvis haunt, with the fervid Rustam Mehta and his bewitching wife Vina. She would make a good fairy-tale sorceress, a Circe waylaying lost voyagers, turning them into captive swine, or whatever. That is unfair, but the thought occurs only because she had been so mesmerizing last night; it is at her bidding, conveyed by the plea in those soft liquid black eyes, that he is back again the next morning. He sights her and her husband sitting on a long sofa at the far end of the living room, in the designated rec area. The table-lamp Elvis stands leering beside her on her other side. Her face lights up immediately she sees him and she hastens forward to greet him.

"So nice you've come," she says, and beckons, "come inside to where we're sitting. It's our lazy hour."

She is in blue jeans and a black sweatshirt, and her hair has apparently recently been washed, falling behind glistening and loose in frizzy waves over her shoulders.

Rusty, wearing a bright red cardigan, fusses with the black-framed bifocals on his nose; they look recent on him and make him look very much the Indian schoolmaster, or the movie version of one. Speaking of which, an Indian movie is playing on the VCR, the scene a police Jeep chasing a suspect into a wheat field. Rusty gets up and shakes hands, says, "Welcome, have a seat." He beckons toward the other person in the room, a silver-haired woman with a very pink face and dressed in Indian shirt and pyjamas, who cannot shift her eyes from the movie. "My mother-in-law," Rusty says. The old lady folds hands in a namasté and Diamond does likewise. She goes back to watching the movie.

"Have some mithai," Vina says, pointing to the tray of sweets on the coffee table, "and I'll bring you some tea— or would you like food—are you hungry—"

"Of course he's hungry, dear, give him lunch."

"It's quite all right," Diamond says, "the mithai will do—"

But that answer is acknowledgement that he's not had lunch, and the matter is settled. Vina disappears to prepare his food.

"Come," Rusty says, putting a hand on Diamond's back, leading him past the kitchen to the dining room. "Ma—" he says to the old lady, "you finish the movie and tell us what happened."

She smiles gratefully at him.

"Doesn't talk much," Rusty says.

"Does she understand English?"

"Yes, but she's embarrassed to speak it in front of strangers."

A delicious spicy aroma wafts in from the kitchen, where Vina is heard clattering her equipment. Soon she appears, cheerfully humming, and lays her offering upon the dining table. Mumbling customary gratitude and apologies, Diamond sets upon the chappati and okra, rice and daal. Rusty goes and puts on an Elvis number before returning to sit at the table with Diamond.

"You're going to get an overdose of Elvis here," Rusty smiles. "I'm sure you don't mind—"

"He's too polite to say if he minds," Vina calls out from the kitchen. "You make sure you don't take advantage of him."

"This house is actually an Elvis shrine—" Rusty continues.

"And should be declared as one," his wife adds, still in the kitchen.

"We have people stopping over from all sorts of places just to see my Elvis memorabilia."

"I'd like to see what you've got," Diamond says politely. There are no Elvis exhibits to look at, except for the Elvis lamp, which is quite grotesque, especially when lighted, as he recalls from last night. But there has to be a sanctum somewhere where Rusty keeps them. Now that must be a sight.

The house, a modest bungalow with its three bed-rooms at the back, is in fact adorned with Indian artifacts, brass and marble on flat tops, and wood and cloth hang-ings, including a red embroidered Krishna playing a flute. The formal, front portion of the living room is set off by a blue and green oriental carpet gracing the white broadloom and three bright Indian miniature paintings on the outer sidewall. In the dining room a couple of ancestors in black and white stare gloomily down at the table from their perch up on a wall.

Rusty watches his guest indulgently for a while, then catching Diamond's eye and unable to hold himself any longer he unleashes a spiel on his favourite subject.

"I've been to conferences in Poland, Croatia, Denmark, even Israel—all devoted to Elvis and his influ-ence. He's taken far more seriously in those countries than here—the c-word is not out of context here . . . as I was telling you yesterday."

It takes Diamond a moment to recall: c for conspiracy.

"From the very beginning—I'm not sure how familiar you are with Elvis's history—" Rusty pauses, goes on, "from the very beginning they tried to neuter him—that's the only word, I'm afraid, because Elvis was pure, unfettered sexual energy—do you know, after his live appearances he would receive threatening phone calls from men? After he appeared on the Steve Allen show—as a dumb cowboy, no less—he said he'd never been so humiliated in his life; Ed Sullivan showed him only from the waist up. But the youngsters loved him, went berserk over his music and his performances. Finally Uncle Sam said 'I want you,' and spirited him away to Germany for two crucial years of his life. All because he was singing and dancing like the blacks and showing white folks how cool that was. 'The coloured folks been singing and playing it just like I'm doin' now . . . for more years than I know.' Those are his words."

Rusty nods to himself, becomes silent for a couple of minutes, then gets up. "Here—come—let me show you something—" They go back to the rec room, sit down beside the cabinet that houses the TV and the stereo system. The Indian movie is over, and old Ma sits brooding, staring at the blank screen. "Go take a rest, Ma," Rusty says gently to her, "there's cooking to be done later, and you shouldn't be tired for that." After a moment's hesitation she wafts away. Rusty unlocks the bottom level of the cabinet and opens both its doors with a flourish: there is a long row of LPs and singles slanting edgewise on a wire rack. He smiles. "Go on, take a look. There are people who'd kill for even a fraction of this treasure."

He begins handing Diamond selected singles to look at, and Diamond takes them gingerly from him, examines them, puts them on the floor beside him. They are old—ancient—some in their thin white inner sleeves only, others with the glossy outer covers intact. Before these 45s, there were the brittle 78 rpms, Diamond recalls.

Bing Crosby, Bill Haley and the Comets, Fats Domino, Ella Fitzgerald, and Elvis, of course. "Wooden Heart," "King Creole," "Don't Be Cruel" . . .

"Can you guess where I got these—most of these—from?"

"Where?"

"Bombay. Some are from my own boyhood collection. Some I bought from junk stores, even street vendors—so much had been simply thrown away. I scoured the streets of Bombay looking for Elvis. I could write a book just on Elvis in Bombay. . . ."

"That'd make a fascinating book," Diamond says.

"You think so?"

"You should write it before someone else does."

Rusty appreciates that, seems touched by it.

"Look at this baby—" he says in a trembling, low voice, eyes shining.

Diamond takes the record. "Hound Dog" by Big Mama Thornton, the first ever recording of the song.

"Elvis did not steal credit for it—from Big Mama—as some people claim," Rusty explains. "On the contrary—everybody else who sang the song, including Bill Haley, simply mushed it up for white audiences. Elvis came along and sang it closest to Big Mama's style—I'll let you hear both and you'll see what I mean. That's tribute, if you ask me. And the same goes for Arthur 'Big Boy' Crudup's 'That's Alright Mama'—you know that one?"

"Only Elvis's version."

Bespectacled, scholarly Rusty—Diamond stares at him, crouched on his knees, handling his collection with the greatest devotion and care. Purely on looks, you might take him for a mathematical whiz, a chess player, a mad scientist. But he is an Elvis expert, knows everything there is to know about Elvis. Others can recite *Macbeth* or *Hamlet*, Keats or Shelley by heart; Alfred Mendelsohn, Diamond's father-in-law, can trace extant first editions like living family relations; Rusty Mehta of Bombay can recite every Elvis song from memory and give you the history of all its performances and recordings.

Rusty has put a hand on Diamond, saying, "I say—sorry, old chap—for going on." The unexpected Briticism is startling: a mannerism from the past, making a sudden, brief reappearance from banishment.

They go back to the dining table for tea. A large variety of mithai—sweetmeats—has been spread out on a tray.

"From my sister in Chicago," Vina says, beaming.

"Tell me," Vina asks a little later, when just the two of them are at the table, "how long are you staying with us?"

"Oh. I'm leaving tomorrow. I hope I've not inconvenienced you—" Had he taken last night's invitation too literally? He is soon disabused of that thought.

"Oh no, it's not that I want you to leave! In fact I wish—I hope—you'll stay longer—" There's a childlike plea in her voice.

"I can't."

"Why?"

Why indeed, because I'd like to be moving along, I can hardly stay in the home of complete strangers more than a night, and even then. . . . But he doesn't know quite how to put that to her.

"Think about it," she says.

He smiles, which could have been taken as polite assent. He feels sorry for her; that wonderful exterior, this show of Indian hospitality that will not take no for an answer, hides a terrible loneliness and isolation after all. She deserves better: masses of people around her, an extended family and friends, in-laws to bicker with, servants to do her work, a community she belongs to.

A place such as this mummifies you at the core, that vital core of your being. You learn the lingo and show off the idiom, use the modern conveniences and say how could you ever have lived back *there*; but all the while that mummy inside you cries out for release. Or you grow warts, get weird....

On a cold and grey Chicago morning...

"Do you know this one?" Rusty asks, having put on a CD.

"Yes," Diamond replies.

Rusty gives him a look that acknowledges, if anything, that the guest is not entirely ignorant. Vina gives a barely perceptible smile.

"Rusty—" she puts in while she has the chance. "Rusty, perhaps we can convince our guest to stay longer—"

"Of course he'll stay—it's not as if he has to rush off to work in the morning," declares Rusty too glibly, then turns to show a more reasonable face to Diamond: "Stay a few days with us. Find out how we live in the Midwest."

"Stay the week, please," begs Vina.

She has lost some of the poise that so charmed him last night; but meanwhile she has revealed a side of herself no less compelling, in that it is intimate and friendly and vulnerable.

"All right, I'll stay tomorrow also but not a day more," he relents and could kick himself for yielding so easily.

Vina sees the look in his eyes and says teasingly, "Tomorrow, at least, to start with."

"Only tomorrow," he says firmly.

"Let Raja decide," Rusty says, observing the exchange indulgently. "You should meet Raja anyway, he'll tell you when you should go."

"Who's Raja?" Is there a dog here he's missed, who influences the household, or perhaps a resident ghost?

"You will find out tomorrow. Now we have to go out for groceries—let's go, Diamond."

"No—let him rest," Vina tells him. "You go by yourself—or take Shireen."

Diamond thanks her with a look.

"I know," she says, putting things away, "you can have a bit too much of Rusty. He's a darling, really."

She goes and puts on a selection of Indian film songs.

"We're going to have an Indian evening—music, biryani, laapsi, kulfi for dessert, and a movie—an oldie. What says you to that?"

"Sounds terrific."

He goes to his basement room and lies down on his back, wondering how he will extricate himself from the tight embrace he has recklessly walked into. Somewhat delicately. He doesn't want to hurt the couple. How familiar he's become with them in such a short time. That's disconcerting. Is *he* the one hungering for closeness? Perhaps it's they who have taken pity on him. He's utterly alone, after all, and drifting like a sea rat. There's nothing, nowhere to return to. His life has gone up in flames.

—*You know I loved you, Di.*

Her plea. She was frightened.

At first it was the recurring colds. Then there appeared the boil on her thigh, the first external sign, grim as a death's head to the knowing. It's not related to HIV, he murmured, when she showed it to him. *It must be,* she whimpered. Shh, he carried her to bed, put her to sleep. And how many more times of that, as the body yielded up one defence then another, a fortress whose doors had suddenly turned to jelly . . . and the rats advanced for the feed. She repulsed him at times, to his horror, and attracted him at others when he saw her as she had been. I would have wished the same for me, he told himself, after all that time together, all the young days we gave each other. I would have liked—not demanded—the same, someone to bathe and clean me, feed and change me, battle my depression, play me music and even sing, hold me through the agony of pain and put me to sleep, as the body quakes and breaks and screams. A complete marriage, through thick and thin, sin and forgiveness, sickness and decay. Is this what it means, through sickness and health, she asked once pathetically, it's so not fair; and he replied, yes, that's what it means to be married and to love, we are for each other. There was no religious dividend, no reward in afterlife that goaded him, there was just that sense of duty, in giving dignity to his partner when the moment demanded. We never bargain for this kind of duty, so when it comes, grab it, it gives some meaning to life. Finally, when it was really impossible to look after her, when the medications were multiple and constant yet producing little hope, he took her—carried her—to the hospital ward. It was then that her parents came and told him, now let her be ours. The next day she died. They cremated her, took the ashes back to New York.

*

He decides to go out for a walk.

The house is built on a wooded hillside and is the last one on a road that heads straight out and up from the local hospital at the edge of town. All the houses are on the same side of the road. A little further up, the road turns to the right and crests before descending to meet the highway exit for Greenfield. The area has the spookiness of a housing development abruptly halted, a town expansion abandoned and forgotten.

As Diamond watches the traffic on the highway from the road crest, he sees Vina walking toward him at a brisk pace.

"It's a good walk," she says when she reaches him, panting lightly. "People ski here in the winter, and do all kinds of winter sport."

They go back together, at a casual pace. She asks to see, and he shows her a picture of Susan that he still carries in his wallet. She looks at it without comment. As they approach the house he asks her, "Where do they burn the cross—the Klan or whoever they are?"

She takes him to a clearing diagonally across from the house; it shows evidence of occupation by builders not long ago—a mound of abandoned sand, a few bricks, bits of PVC piping, an empty reel of electrical cord.

"They've come twice," she tells him. "They parked here on the road and came out of their trucks wearing white hoods. We thought they looked funny at first, and there must be a mistake. It looked like a Halloween night. But then they stood facing the house, and making strange sounds—hooting and howling—and filthy, abusive comments. We were terrified. The second time they brought out a tall white cross. . . ."

"Have they harassed other non-whites in the area?"

"No. Only us. It has to do with Elvis. You should ask Rusty. We hope they'll stop, get tired or something. It's driving us—and him especially—crazy."

"And the police—what did they say?"

"By the time they finished questioning us on the phone, the hoods had gone."

"When was the last time they came—these hoods?"

"Over two months ago."

III.

*Rustam Mehta, shaking uncon-*trollably, begins stamping a foot and mouthing a stream of obscenities he cannot be quite conscious of, as he stands glaring out the picture window at the spectacle taking place outside. The drapes were overlooked earlier and are open. A helpless, tearful Vina hovers beside her husband, unable to calm him.

They had entered the second hour of the long Indian film, had taken their dessert and tea was to follow shortly, when Rusty suddenly sat up and stiffened, adjusted his glasses, and before anyone could respond was up and running to the window, shouting, "It's them! They're here!"

"Who, what?" Diamond said, startled, no sooner having asked which than he heard the low humming of truck engines outside. Vina was already up, behind Rusty, and Shireen emerged from the privacy of her room.

Two trucks, engines on, headlights off, parked across the road from the house; six hooded Klan figures, four of them strutting about, evidently up to something, the other two standing erect, arms folded, facing the house. A white cross about five feet long appears, held up vertically by two of the four figures, apparently burning but actually powered electrically by one of the truck batteries. Tepid, smoke-free Klansmen (and perhaps women), to the townspeople a joke in bad taste.

There comes a look of terror on Vina's face at the sight of the raised fluorescent cross; her face drained white, she turns her large eyes silently upon Diamond. Her husband, on the other hand, in constant fidgety motion, is red with rage. The old woman is next to Diamond, moaning, perhaps uttering invocations, and he feels compelled to put an arm around her frail shoulders. Shireen watches all with a calm, blank face, all her expression caught in her tense young body, her fists clenched at her sides. Diamond's eyes meet the girl's and he wants to apologize, say to her, Sorry kid, I'm so sorry, we should be able to do something.

Rusty meanwhile has dashed off inside and emerged waving a handgun in front of him, screaming, "I'll show them, those motherfuckers—"

His wife moves to restrain him, "No, Rusty, please, this isn't the solution, Rusty—"

Rusty, "Get out of my way," is back at the window yelling mindless imprecations. "Come out you yellow bastards, redneck devils! Halloween ghosts, mahdder chod, show your balls you cowards in bedsheets!"

In reply, mindless answers, mock laughter: "Tee-hee,

tee-hee," and what Diamond discerns as "Go home, nig-gers," and "Elvis ain't for Hin-doo cows—tee-hee."

There comes the faint sound of music from a truck radio; perhaps Elvis.

The Indian movie, still running in the rec area behind them, belongs to another world.

Rusty is finally subdued, the trucks speed away. The terror has lasted ten minutes.

Rusty, gasping for breath, is guided to a sofa, and he hands his gun to Vina, who with a doubtful glance at it passes it quickly to Diamond. It is the first time Diamond has held a gun, and somewhat alarmed at himself he can't suppress a twinge of excitement, a trite momentousness, at the feel of its compact metallic black density in his hands; it is an object, he surmises with grudging admira-tion—turning it around and over, running his fingers over the grip with the maker's insignia, the smooth bar-rel, all the notches, the grooves, the sleek multiple surfaces in such a small space—designed and finished with devotion. It looks perfect.

"It's a cool weapon—Beretta 92, double-action 9-mm auto, packs ten shells in all of two pounds," says Shireen.

In the frenzy of the past few minutes she had disap-peared from sight. Here she is now in her denim and khaki, tall and limber, a rifle held casually in one hand.

"Isn't that too heavy for you?" he asks for want of any-thing better to say.

"Nope. It's mine, a ladies' model—Winchester."

She lets him hold it.

IV.

Next morning brings a calm bright cheeriness with it, the household taken over in happy preoccupation with its weekend routines—Vina and her mother cooking brunch, Shireen watching cartoons, Rusty pottering away in the backyard; and the previous night's terror a bad dream.

"Here's the *Chicago Tribune*," says Vina, as Diamond emerges from his basement domain. She indicates the paper on the dining table and brings over a cup of tea along with a plate of sweets from the kitchen. "Brunch will be a while yet." He smiles his thanks and she sits down a moment with him. She is still in her housecoat, a fact that sends an unwelcome pang of nostalgia through him. The plain, unmade face has a nice frankness to it, and the multiple loose strands from her casually tied hair make her viscerally attractive. Feeling his predatory look upon her, she skips away with a knowing smile.

A sizzling overture precedes the aroma of fried spices that soon begins to fill the air. In the background the kitchen TV contends boisterously with a program of ear-catching Indian oldies from the films of the sixties. "The program comes to us on cable from Vancouver," Vina explains. "Come inside the kitchen if you would like to watch the show."

He would hate to watch old black-and-white dance numbers from a bygone era, and he declines the invitation politely, saying he'd rather not crowd the kitchen more than it already is, with both Ma and Vina busy inside. The hostess nods she understands. Taking the paper with him, hunting for a suitable place to read by himself, Diamond pauses briefly at the front window. Cool golden sunlight bathes the earth on this beautiful, peaceful fall Sunday as serene as the first day of creation. Did this same world on some nights grow horns, wings, and scales, breathe fire and howl to terrify the inhabitants of this house?

Vina has to announce brunch in several parts of the house before everyone gathers at the table. There is on offer puri and spiced potato garnished with fresh coriander, which Ma grew indoors, and parathas stuffed with radishes and other vegetables, an omelette, and idlies and daal. Altogether a meal for a platoon, Diamond observes, and Ma says something that Vina relays as, "We have to fatten you up." Rusty reassures him, "You'll use it all up. I'd like you to help me in the backyard for a while."

Afterwards Vina, Ma, and Shireen pick up the telephones for their Sunday call-up-long-distance ritual, and Rusty and Diamond go to work in the backyard. The women have cleaned up the vegetable and flower gardens and replenished the soil, the grass is trim; now it is up to the man to fortify the castle against the coming cold season. With his guest's compliant though unskilled assistance he repairs a wire fence (under which a fox has persistently burrowed that year) and a storm door, replaces storm windows, cleans up and resecures the kitchen exhaust vent where a family of birds had nested in the summer. He works fast and intensely, breathing hard and grunting from the exertions. "Back home we disdained such work," Rusty says, "here we take pride in it."

In the three hours of labour Rusty pointedly avoids the most conspicuous part of the backyard, and Diamond avoids asking him about it; finally they proceed toward it.

The path of inlaid stone, approaching directly from the side door on the right of the house, proceeds at the back toward a small square building the size of an average room. It has a light blue stucco exterior and an arched studded door under a facade shaped like the section of a dome. A flower bed runs around its sides, in portions of which the two men as their final chore devotedly plant tulips to blossom next spring.

Having finished, they stand back and appraise each other. Diamond waits for the explanation he has already guessed.

"This is my shrine to Elvis Raja," Rusty says. "Let's wash up and come back."

But before returning they have an elaborate afternoon tea with the family, an Indian custom that cannot be violated.

Rusty waits for him to step inside, then closes the door and turns on the lights. Diamond draws a sharp breath of astonishment; a multitude of colours and images leap out all around him, assaulting his senses.

It's a picture of Rustam Mehta's brain, he tells himself, after a moment's pause; if you want to know what's inside it, this is it, this dizzying madness of blatant multi-coloured fantasies . . . and he belongs to another planet, surely.

The floor is wood, covered in plush white broadloom. There is a smell of paint and carpet, intermingled with incense. Rusty takes off his shoes on a mat just inside the entrance and motions for his guest to do the same, after which they proceed forward. The ceiling is painted in a geometrical design of alternate blue and beige lines radiating from the centre, to create a crude illusion of the inside of a dome. The wall to their left bustles with myriad miniature Elvis hand paintings. The right wall contains an incomplete mural. And straight ahead lies the sanctum sanctorum of this temple. In the centre of the wall is a large, circular head-and-shoulder portrait of late Elvis painstakingly constructed from chips of tile. "Vina's handiwork," Rusty whispers. Around this portrait runs a border containing the words "Elvis King of the World" as well as two words in Hindi script that Diamond can't read. Bright yellow rays radiate from the central image to the four edges of the wall.

"And look here," Rusty says in his low voice, taking a diagonal step to his right and kneeling down.

On the floor, on a bit of maroon carpet, stand four gaudily painted cutout figures of wood or cardboard. Diamond's heart flutters as he too kneels to view them fully—they look like Hindu icons, each with the face of Elvis. Elephant-headed pot-bellied Ganesh, with puffy middle-aged, perhaps drug-drenched, Elvis face and leer, the trunk holding a small guitar; monkey-god Hanuman as the rock 'n' rolling young Elvis in hound-dog pelvis-shaking posture; blue Krishna holding a mike and proffering a benevolent smile; and finally, in the centre, larger than the rest by a head, a black Elvis as Kali the terrible in her dance of death, gorged on blood and guts, her two arms falling over a guitar slung across the neck, and at her feet the skulls of vanquished foes—identified in small handwritten red print as Andy Williams, Bing Crosby, John, Paul, George, and Ringo.

Away from these four Elvis-as-god icons, to their right, stands a squat stubby silo-like phallus of grey stone, at the tip of which plays a white jumpsuited Elvis with pink face and hands; singing what—Diamond asks himself—"Love Me Tender"?

Diamond stares at this vision for a long time. He does not know how to respond. It offends, profoundly, yet he isn't sure how. He turns to look at Rusty, who is going on in dead earnestness, "I had these made in India. It was some job bringing them over intact. What do you think?" He looks puzzled by Diamond's silence, but says, "Here, take a look at these—"

An Elvis jumpsuit, white, gold, and silver, hangs ghostlike from a black Ikea coatstand behind the phallus.

"The King himself wore that, at a concert in Iowa City," explains Rusty. "I bought it off the widow of the concert-hall manager . . . didn't come cheap, but I beat a competitor to it. And now, here's some more memorabilia—"

He heads toward a tall, narrow table almost exactly at the centre of the room. Upon it rests a shallow glass case containing an odd assortment of objects: a red, white, and blue neck scarf, still wrinkled at the two ends where it had presumably been tied; a silver button sewn to a piece of white cloth, a lock of black hair, a short length of wire that could be from a guitar string, a shard from a broken singles record, a comb, a jockstrap; a small test tube containing a brown waxlike substance. . . .

"Don't ask me how I got that button—it's from a suit Elvis wore during a concert—after which he gave it to his cousin Gene to hold, then Gene missed his limousine and was chased by a frenzied mob down a street, and finally in desperation he threw the whole expensive suit at them. . . ."

He falls silent, watches Diamond contemplate the entire room from this central vantage point. Leaving Diamond at the table, he hurries over to the icons in front and lights some incense, and somewhere else he puts on an Elvis version of a gospel song, before returning.

"Impressed?" he asks. "What do you think?"

"Yes, I am impressed," Diamond replies, "I truly am, by all this," and Rusty glows with emotion.

"You know—" he says, hesitantly, putting a hand on Diamond's arm. "I have a . . . a dream—don't laugh, please—a dream that in a few decades—perhaps half a century—Elvis will be at the centre of a new world religion that will contain all the other religions. He speaks to so many people from all backgrounds and ages—even in different languages. What was Jesus when *he* started out? Elvis is much more. And look at the condition of the world today—the hunger and greed . . . wars and massacres . . . all the intolerance . . . Now more than ever we need Elvis. Have you noticed, the letters of his name can be rearranged to read: LIVES?"

No, Diamond says, he hadn't noticed that. They go to examine the left wall.

"This wall is the work of Ma. She used to be an art teacher in India. For several months every morning she would come here and create one image of Elvis."

Hundreds of Elvises, from straight copies of movie posters to far-out fantasies—Elvis as Arab prophet kneeling before the angel Gabriel holding in front of him a musical score, Elvis as baby Jesus, Elvis riding on a tiger, Elvis with a beard.

The incomplete mural on the opposite wall is planned to depict a procession set against a red background, in a desert perhaps, as an allegory of the three stages of life.

"This is my work. I'm afraid I'm not a very good artist . . ."

"I'm sure Raja says I can go now," Diamond says and smiles as graciously as he can at his hosts. He feels nervous and edgy after the recent experience. Am I in a nuthouse, he asks himself. The three of them have gathered at the dining table. From the TV comes the rasp of pro football commentary.

"Raja will tell us after dinner," Rusty says, pleased with Diamond's remark.

The phone rings, Rusty goes and picks it up.

Vina says in the interlude, "It's so nice you're here. How did you find Rusty's museum, hmm?"

"A little too strong for my taste," Diamond murmurs.

"It's his thing," she replies softly. "We all need our own madness, don't we, in order to survive?"

He looks sharply at her, and she puts her hand on his arm, and he thinks, Would you like to be my madness? She pulls her arm away.

"That portrait you made for the shrine is very good," he says.

"We all pitched in."

"By the way," Diamond says to Rusty coming back from the phone. "Who is Raja?"

Rusty stops, and says, "Oh. I thought you knew. Didn't we tell you?"

"No," says Diamond. "An oracle of sorts?"

"An oracle, yes. *Raja*, my dear friend, is exactly that— King. And who is the King?—*He don't stop playing till his guitar breaks* . . . Elvis, of course," Rusty proclaims and traipses onward to his chair.

"You don't mean—" Diamond sputters helplessly at Vina.

She comforts him, "We'll conduct a seance. Don't worry. It's quite harmless—and so revealing, you'll see."

There is a short silence, as the couple let him absorb the information. Then Vina says, "My sister Rina's coming over Tuesday—day after tomorrow. I'd like you to meet her, Diamond. You'll like her. She's a beautician— and quite a beauty herself, isn't she, Rusty? I was always the ugly duckling in the family," she smiles.

That must make me a Frankenstein, Diamond thinks glumly. He takes the photo Vina passes him, of herself and her sister Rina, in full pose, in red and blue saris. Yes, the sister is pretty, though a little too tall and forlorn looking, and she doesn't hold a candle to you my dear, he thinks, meeting Vina's eye.

"She is divorced," Vina says, attempting innocence, "and no children. I do think you should meet her."

He goes for a long walk. His Ford Escort is now parked further into the driveway—Vina had asked to move it, now her car is parked behind his. And Vina has his keys. How will he get away if Raja rules against his leaving?

Will this place be his prison? He walks up the hill, then comes down to the highway exit, to walk back to the house from the town side. On his way downhill a four-wheel drive passes him at full speed, the two occupants letting off a howl in his vicinity. He wonders if the two are among the Mehtas' tormenters. Hasn't anyone thought of taking down licence-plate numbers, or even taking a video of the scene?

v.

After dinner the Parker Brothers Ouija board is brought out onto the cleared dining table, and all take their seats and gather around. The light is dimmed, and letters, numbers, and symbols begin to glow in the semi-dark, as if imbued with their own independent mysterious energy. The planchette is a flat yellow heart-shaped piece of plastic on three stubby legs, with a circular viewing window in the centre. Rusty says, "Move closer, everybody—now the procedure is this: you take hold of the planchette, very lightly, at the edge, with your fingers—you may even just touch it. And with your free hand grab someone else's free hand—the energy is strong today, there's all the day's anticipation focused on this . . . ," he pauses, ". . . on this hour. Ready, now?"

"Yes, let's begin—" Vina says, giving a shiver of delight, and everybody dutifully places their fingers on the planchette. First Rusty, then Vina, Diamond, and Shireen. Ma is too old to lean forward like the others and simply places a hand on her granddaughter's shoulder.

Already the object seems charged with energy, hopping nervously about and raring to go. "Grab somebody's hand," Vina says, taking Diamond's beside her.

"Are you there—who is it—" Rusty queries in a high pitch.

Judging by Rusty's voice, whatever it is, if anything, has to be five or six feet away, Diamond estimates, but he feels no flutter of excitement, no suspense, no supernatural vibrations in the air—or is it ether, he wonders, in this context? He allows his hand to be carried along with the others' by the planchette as it jumps and slides about before landing on "A."

"No, I want to communicate with Raja, are you there, Raja?"

But "A" is persistent; he turns out to be Asim, and he has a message for Nafisa; he still loves her. Having delivered this message, not saying who or where Nafisa is, Asim leaves. There is a long pause. Diamond senses Vina's hand, soft and pliable in his, and he squeezes it. There is no resistance.

The planchette gives a start.

"Is that you, Raja?" Rusty asks intensely, losing no time.

Pause, then the planchette hops over to the "Yes" box.

"Oh wonderful!" Vina exclaims with relief, and next to Shireen, Ma emits a chuckle.

Rusty continues, "Thank you, Elvis Raja, do you have something to say first?"

Yes. The little heart waddles off to spell out S-O-N-G. . . .

"Song?" Yes. "You're asking *me* to sing—you'll never give up, will you? All right, Raja, I'll indulge you."

Rusty gives a quick look around at the others. Then he sings a high-pitched off-tune version of "Crying in the Chapel," mercifully stopping after a few lines.

"I'm not as good as you, Raja, and you do like to tease me."

"What else, Raja?" Vina jumps in.

"Hurry up," Rusty whispers, "you know he doesn't have much time—he gets hundreds of summonses all the time."

"Tell us about those men in hoods who harass us so much," Vina speaks, in a spoiled little-sister voice.

The little heart on the board tilts, then hops along.

"D-O . . . ," Vina reads out. "Mr. Doris the teacher—okay. Can you tell us of anyone else? . . . He always gives only that one name," she whispers to Diamond. "I wonder why. . . ."

The planchette is still. The old woman stirs, mumbles something.

"Okay, Ma," says Shireen. "Raja, tell Ma how is Manek —her husband and my grandfather."

She could be talking to a dog in that tone, Diamond thinks.

The heart tips a few times on its legs but declines to spell out a message.

"He is well and sends greetings," Rusty says, too quickly; then adds: "Well, we *know* he's doing well where he is."

"He's reborn as a little girl in a fabulously rich household in Mysore," Shireen says to no one in particular. "Isn't that what Raja told us the other time?"

"Let's ask him our question before he leaves," Rusty says in a low voice, then speaks up, "Okay, here's the big question, Raja—you can't sign off without answering this one—"

Vina takes over, sounding anxious: "Should we allow Diamond, our guest, to leave tomorrow morning . . . or do you think he should stay longer and. . . ." Her grip on Diamond's hand tightens, he responds instinctively.

Without hesitation the planchette hobbles off energetically on its three legs to spell out S-T-A-Y.

"Stay! That's unequivocal," concludes Rusty firmly. "The guest will stay a few days more."

Diamond feels not only a tight squeeze on his hand but also the bite of a nail. The yellow heart on the board runs off to "Yes," then starts tilting back and forth and suddenly stops.

"He's gone," Rusty says softly, then calls out, "'Bye, Raja. You're still King and we love you."

They sit back in their chairs and give a collective sigh. Someone turns the light back to bright. The old woman smiles contentedly, and Shireen is beaming. And Diamond feels duped.

"Well?" Rusty looks around.

"Shall we continue," Vina says, "or shall I put the tea on?"

The planchette is on the board, Rusty touches it lightly with a forefinger. It jumps.

"Let's see who it is, I feel the energy, it's especially high today . . . must be you, Diamond."

Sure it's me, Diamond thinks ruefully.

Rusty dims the light.

"Okay now—pay attention. . . ."

Stillness, again, anticipation, hands held; and the planchette begins to hobble in the false twilight. But it cannot find a resting place. Rusty deals with the presence sternly.

"Who are you? Identify yourself, please. Who do you want to speak to?"

P-E-G . . . And Diamond's heart stops. *Peggy-Peggy-Peggy, my Peggy-Sue . . .*

"Who's Peg?" Rusty inquires. "Who do you want to speak to, Peg?"

Vina throws a quick glance at Diamond, says, "No one we know. Sign off then, Rusty."

They let go their hands.

—*I loved you, Di. . . .*

—*I know, and I loved you too, Sue.*

Vina stands up, beaming. "So you're not going," she says to Diamond. "I'm so glad."

"Yes. Raja has spoken," Rusty says. "You know, once he disputed the content of my course with me—he didn't like my interpretation of one of his songs. I told him, 'Lay off, Raja, once an artist's done his work, it belongs to the audience—and the critic. It's no longer yours.' He took no offence."

Diamond feels he's been clobbered on the head. Thanks to Raja, he will have to tarry a while longer at this place; but how much longer? He recalls that his car is blocked, and his key is with Vina. Meanwhile she has invited her tall, pretty sister to come and meet him, this nice single man from Toronto, whom she's also been teasing; if he doesn't watch himself, he could end up married a second time, living in Chicago and related to the Mehtas. The family, the three adults, must surely have discussed this prospect amongst themselves; Ma already took a proprietorial tone regarding him this morning, talking of fattening him up.

He excuses himself, telling his hosts he'll skip dinner and retire early tonight, and goes down to his room. He feels tired, as perhaps everybody else does after the seance. He doesn't believe in spirits that live on after death and communicate with humans, but the session with the Ouija board had been intense and draining. He has no doubt, however, that the Mehtas have forced their collective will on him, using a game they play seriously.

And what of Sue's presence at the tail end of the session? He must have guided the planchette on the board himself, spelling out his nickname for her, in a desperate desire to speak with her; sensing this, Vina had rather quickly dismissed "Peg" as someone of no importance.

What would he have asked her?

Diamond is embarrassed at himself, at his seduction by the game board and the putative power of the yellow hobbling heart. For a moment, he had let his guard down, he who has never believed in finding fortunes in stars or palms or tea leaves. He smiles. Sue would have enjoyed this. Sue is dead. Sue is not a spirit.

She had been Rationality itself. A degree in philosophy, studied Spinoza for a while, but didn't have the energy for a doctorate. And so she took up employment at Ontario's Ministry of Culture. It was through that work that she met the gay Indian dancer Payal, who also ran a seashell gallery. Payal had a wealthy partner, Christopher, twenty years his senior. Christopher died of HIV and Payal needed a lot of comforting. But it was Payal's friend

Henry, another Indian, who became Sue's fatal attraction.

—How could you, Sue?

—You forget that you were depressed, Di. That's not an excuse, but it was hard for me. You wanted to let everything go and travel the world by yourself, to Borneo and the Seychelles and Cape Horn you said, simply to fulfill a childhood dream. You would tell me about incidents from your school days that had no meaning for me. On and on, Di . . . and I was frightened for you, for us. I'm not justifying, Di, I'm not. All that time together, Di. . . .

—Yes, all that time together, Sue. You taught me how to read Schopenhauer, and you made me sit down, you and your father Max, and listen to Beethoven, and you read The Song of Solomon *to me . . . this innocent abroad . . . and I told you I was so happy to be alive in this world full of beauty and excitement, this world that contained you . . . I recall how during the blackout of '79 Max and I went searching for you in the Bronx, Max hiding a baseball bat inside his jacket. . . . The betrayal was not in that silly bit of unfaithfulness, Sue, it was in catching that death so carelessly. . . .*

He has been lying down on his back, in the dark, and fallen asleep in his clothes. He is startled awake by the squeak of the door and sits up; a tall dark figure, a silhouette stands framed at the open doorway. For a terror-filled moment he stares at it, dumbstruck, clutching at the bedclothes, before the overhead light goes on. It is Shireen. Quickly she is inside, has closed the door behind her. His heart is thudding as he watches her, relieved and struggling to muster amusement from the fright she's just given him. By his watch it is eleven. And what does she want, this girl?

She comes and stands before him.

"You want to make your escape, right?"

He looks at her in confusion.

"As in vamoose, split, take a powder—from this god-forsaken place?"

He nods with a grin. "Yes."

She brings a hand from behind her, throws him his car key.

"I've moved Mom's car from behind yours—the road's clear. Make your escape when they're all asleep."

"Thank you," he says. He doesn't know what else to say. He hasn't got to know her. She makes for the door.

"I'll stay in touch," he says hastily. "And don't do anything foolish—" He recalls her with her rifle.

"Great," she says and closes the door behind her.

At four a.m. his little quartz alarm clock gives a beep and wakes him, and he quietly dresses and tiptoes out with his bag. He has to take his chances. Even the rustle of clothing or the tiny click of the front door shutting, magnified by the hour, could awaken a restless sleeper and humiliate him in midstride. Happily, all of the bedrooms are at the back.

The engine turns with monstrous disregard for the vast silence all around it. He carefully backs out into the road and drives off, heading for the highway exit. It is possible, he thinks, that he did see a female figure standing at the front window, watching him in the darkness. In any case, how did Shireen obtain his key from her mom? Perhaps Vina simply decided to overrule Raja, and her own instincts, and let him go.

The Trouble with Tea

Having removed his shoes in the shoes-and-coat corner at the far end of the long, shadowy corridor, he retraced his steps partway and came to the brightly lit anteroom, which he entered, proceeding straight for the tea counter. It was high and wide, Formica topped, dividing the large room in half. The young woman on the other side gave a brief smile and wordlessly poured his tea from a kettle into one of the odd assortment of cups she had neatly arrayed before her on a grey metal tray.

On his side the room was bare, but for the low wooden benches along the three walls. Two people occupied the benches, sitting across from each other: a thin young man and a middle-aged woman, sipping in silence. The other door from this room opened into the dark cavern of the prayer hall. Taking his cup, he took a seat against the third, unoccupied wall, between the man and the woman, and took his first small taste of the tea.

It was, he thought—this early, four-in-the-morning cup of tea, strong, creamy, sweet—the best you could find. The miracle was, it was the same everywhere, in Dar es Salaam, in Vancouver, and here on Dundas Street, Toronto; what's more, this soothing morning cup had been the same from as far back in his life as he could remember, even in its temperature. It scalded the tongue if you took a large sip right away, but even then not too severely. Taken in small sips at the right pace, it was pleasantly hot in the mouth and refreshing to the mind.

It was as if the formula, passed on for generations, had now spread to the four corners of the earth, and here he was, in one such corner, a yellow oil-painted room in a converted supermarket at Dundas and Bloor, partaking of the rich potion in the company of two other devotees before he went into the dark prayer hall for meditation.

You could tell the taste anywhere but, as everyone knew, you could find it only in mosque and only in its morning session, between four and five. And so it was called the tea of the morning session. It was taken always in silence, not a word was uttered even if the tea room was full, as it was on certain days. This was after all the period when men and women had given up the sweetest part of their sleep to come in quest of the eternal. An occasional tinkle from a cup was indulged, a rustle of clothing when someone arrived could not be helped. The barest trace of a perfume.

And yet, this sweet blameless cup of tea had been under attack ever since his childhood. Tea was not healthy, its accusers would pronounce; it made the mind wander; some people came only for the taste of the tea and forgot all about the sanctity of the hour, the well-being of their souls. These complaints had long been heard and duly received their nods of dutiful assent. Everyone agreed, how could they not? But the custom of providing the tea and consuming it had gone on, year after year. To give up the tea! Unthinkable.

Now here too, in Toronto, murmurs had arisen against the morning cup. In this new environment where so many of the old ways had died, would this tea—this special chai—survive? The first battle of the tea had already been fought, a few months before, and won. In the York Mills mosque, a young doctor had assumed the position of mukhi, the presider. One of his first decisions upon taking over was a health experiment. For a few days he did away with the tea and served glasses of cool water instead. Within a matter of days he had seen the light, having realized it would not be long before he found himself alone in a dark empty hall. The beloved brew was brought back.

He went into the prayer hall. Pleasantly carpeted, peace-fully—not menacingly—dark, its space seemed laden with a spiritual presence, perhaps emanating collectively from the souls meditating inside. Or perhaps this was simply an effect simulated by the soft glow of the several nightlights in the hall. Long ago, and elsewhere, there had been no nightlights, you simply let your eyes adjust gradually to the darkness and make out the shadowy figures seated on the floor, dispersed variously, among which you meandered your way and picked your place to sit. Accidents happened—or, to be honest, had been reported to have happened. As when a man stumbled and fell upon a sitting woman, who protested indignantly, breaking the dead silence with a sudden "Don't you have any shame?" That was a joke to bring on the giggles any time. Or, when the lights came on one morning at the end of the meditation hour, a man found himself, red-faced, sitting in the midst of tittering women.

He was smiling at these recollections, these jokes of his youth, when he found his regular spot and lowered himself against a wall.

People, being creatures of habit, arrived at their own set times and found their own regular places to sit in the dark, so from day to day this hall looked the same, sounded the same—the cough, the sigh, the snore, the rustle of clothing. When the lights came on, you would match the scene now revealed before you with the shapes, the sounds, and other goings-on of the dark hour, and if a familiar pattern had been broken you would confirm who came late, who gave the untoward moan or snort, who the new face was in a place reserved by convention for someone else. A comradeship formed of these early morning seekers, though not much was said among

them, and even old acquaintances exchanged few words;
if you were not seen for a few days you would definitely
be missed.

Only the hardiest—and the true—among the devotees came at this hour. You did not give up sleep at its
sweetest to drive down a Bloor Street West emptied of
all life except the police cars (and what were *they* up to,
in those numbers, at that hour?), the occasional drunk,
and the all-night doughnut store, simply for appearance.
You came to fight a private battle with yourself, find the
inner self, see the light. To meditate on the mantra, the
word, the two-syllable name of God, in-out with the
breath, until you became one with it. Some said that
there was a special method of breathing, so that a coil of
energy moved up from the base of the spine to the head.
Others believed in sitting upright like a yogi, and they
looked disdainfully upon those who slouched or used a
wall for support.

But he simply leaned against the wall where he sat,
feet stretched out in front of him, and went in-out with his
breath. Come what may. If he was going to nod off, it had
rather be against a wall, away from all gazes except his
neighbours'. Falling into a nap once in a while was embarrassing but not really shameful and not so uncommon.

Beat the mind and reach the goal, as the old adage
advised. Mind was the enemy. Holding it down was like
trying to catch the wind in your hands. The important
thoughts were easy to put to rest—for now—the wife,
the various debts, the boy doing brilliantly in school ...
until recently ... the girl gone away to Chicago to join an
African-American music group.... When all these larger

preoccupations of daily life had been caught and subdued, it was the little thoughts that refused to lie still. You started thinking about them, how elusive and trivial they were, and soon you were thinking about thinking, and so on.

There. Absolute stillness.

That was hard to achieve.

At times you became conscious of your body trying to relax. You crossed and uncrossed your legs.

One day, in Gujarat in ancient times, a message came to a king called Raja Manshudh, commanding him to bring his presence before his spiritual lord. He was to take his queen with him, but not their infant son. And so early at dawn the next day the king and queen set off on a journey to see their lord. Their way took them upon long trails through forests and woods, the king leading and his wife following faithfully behind, tired and pining for her absent baby. Emerging into a clearing once, the couple came upon a female deer under a small tree, suckling her little one. The sad queen, her breasts gorged with her own milk, collapsed at this reminder of her child and died on the spot. Undeterred, the stalwart king picked up his wife on his shoulder and continued on his voyage till the end, where he presented himself and his dead queen before the master. The lord was pleased and rewarded Raja Manshudh. The queen came alive and the child was brought back into her arms.

The story was an allegory, he had heard it explained as a child. The king was our soul, and the journey was the meditation hour, in which the soul set off to be united with the Universal Soul; the queen was the fickle, desiring part of the mind, what we call the heart, and the child was all that was dear to the heart. Beat, kill the wavering mind and reach the goal, the truth.

What was this truth? It was wisdom, enlightenment, revelation. It was often likened to, it was called, "the light." But it wasn't a real light, like that of a lamp, as the gurus and pirs had always taken pains to explain. It was something that, once you found it, you simply knew. And once you knew it, you couldn't explain it, had no desire to explain it, or even tell anybody that you had seen it. Just as when a poor deaf-mute sees a beautiful moon on a clear breezy night over the trees and has no words to describe the miracle.

Moreover, this enlightenment, the light that was not a light, was not something like a diploma you acquired after completion of a course. It was not a right, but a benediction. You could meditate a lifetime yet not acquire it . . . a depressing thought. And here he was giving sermons to himself again, if he wasn't careful the hour would slip away. . . .

But what would it be like, to have seen the light, experienced that darshan?

Once, back in Dar es Salaam, a certain well-known elder of the community was on his way to morning session. He was one of those—and there were many in those days—who never missed this blessed hour, come what may. Outside his house there would usually be some trucks parked for the night, on the pavement and on the road. As he was hurrying through the deep shadows cast by the trucks, the elder was blinded by an intense light. The poor man, thinking he'd finally been blessed, cried out thankfully, "Praise God! Praise God!" The light went out and a voice said in the dark, "What's wrong, Mister?" It was a night watchman with a flashlight.

It was hard to keep away the silly smile every time the man came to mind; though the incident was probably exaggerated or untrue. He had died recently, in Calgary . . . and what a great singer of hymns he had been back then. . . .

Beat, kill the mind. . . . He sensed people stirring around him in their various places, and it seemed the hour was rapidly approaching its end. Soon it would be another futile hour, to pile up on all those other dead hours, wasted on empty thoughts running ahead of him this way and that, leading him astray. Perhaps it was the tea—that sweet, strong, creamy tea that left such a pleasant taste and a slight odour in the mouth—that excited the mind, made it flit about from thought to thought until one became weary keeping track of them. Perhaps they were right, those critics of the tea . . . but what would it be like, morning mosque without its special tea? Would he come then, spend a good portion of the hour waiting for something to happen to his soul?

His heart at this time, it seemed to him, would always pick up a beat, as though racing now against the few minutes left to the darkness.

Stillness.

He thought, fewer and fewer people show up in the morning these days. His eyes opened momentarily to seek confirmation. The old charm is definitely going, and winter doesn't help any.

This past summer, it was rumoured, a ghost had been

keeping people away. A policeman ghost. The numbers had never completely recovered since then.

Just after you came out of the dark underpass on Bloor West, on the top of the hill, a policeman standing beside a patrol car would wave you down. You stopped. "Your licence, sir. Your insurance." The usual stuff. He would take a walk around the car as though inspecting it. The next thing you knew, he had vanished, and so had the patrol car, and when you got to mosque it was late. The same policeman, every time. Young, tall, blue-eyed. Once a smart aleck attempted to get out of the car but the door wouldn't open. Another time the policeman said, "Follow me," to a man and his wife, who followed him all the way to the airport, but once there, at the arrivals terminal, they saw themselves tagging along behind a taxi.

There had been quite some excitement in those few weeks when the ghost appeared. It seemed that Satan had singled out their simple Dundas mosque for attention, and the morning session would have to be cancelled.

And then a famous preacher, called "Missionary," had volunteered to drive away the policeman ghost. For a few days, at a little after four in the morning, Missionary was driven along Bloor Street on the way to the mosque. Three days nothing happened. On the fourth morning, so the story went, the car was stopped. Missionary rolled down his window and spoke to the cop who had appeared. "Sir, I believe this is what you are looking for." He gave the policeman a folded card, which the policeman took silently and went away. And was never seen again.

This famous incident should have brought hordes of people to morning session, revived flagging faith, but it hadn't. There were even people who denied it ever happened like that.

It had happened in August, the one month he had been away with the family in Calgary, where they had gone to visit his brother and sister and their families. When he returned, it was all over. He wished he had been here, had met the ghost. Bloor Street West was his daily route, after all. But he'd missed the entire episode—the policeman ghost, the exorcism. His life was ordinary, his struggle ordinary—against his cluttered mind and the anxieties about his son and daughter. It seemed to him that he had been created, allotted his portion of worries, and forgotten.

Once Abou ben Adhem (he recalled from a poem he had studied in school) awoke in the middle of the night to see an angel beside him with a scroll and pen in his hands. "What are you writing?" Abou asked. "The names of the people who remember God the most," the angel replied. But Abou's name was not one of them. Disappointed, he went back to sleep. The next night he again saw the angel, writing on a scroll. "What this time?" asked Abou. "The names of the people whom God remembers the most," came the answer. Abou ben Adhem's name was first among these.

No, he wasn't one whom God remembered. His meditations every morning at the hour of four—breathing in-out and repeating the sacred syllables—and all his attempts at stillness, were fruitless, his mind only jangled with useless thoughts. Oh, kill the mind . . . he opened his eyes, gave a quick look around, instinctively, and closed his eyes again.

He opened them and saw that the lights had come on, must have been on for some time; all the ceremonies following the meditation hour were over, he was alone in the brilliantly lit hall, everyone else was out in the tea room. No one had thought to wake him up. People had observed him sitting erect, head lowered, legs folded under him, breathing calmly, in-out. And he, getting up now, did not feel as if he had been asleep.

He came out calm, without the feeling he had wasted another day; he declined more tea and conversation, put on his shoes, and drove home.

If it had been you or I, we would have wondered if this state of grace was real, how long it would last, and if it would reappear the next day. That thought did not occur to him.

Dear Khatija

A Partition Story

LAKSHMI

Among my mother's effects is this brown cardboard box, bursting at the seams, barely held together with a string running all around, drawing the sides in. It's her hoard of old photographs from under her bed. The newer, cheery ones, those of her children—me and my brother Mohan—and her husband and herself, went into the family albums for the viewing benefit of our guests over the years. In this dusty trove of her private memories, stamp-sized snapshots, the personalities of their subjects squeezed into tiny mouse faces, jostle with larger photos that failed to make it to, or perhaps lost their place on, a wall or a dresser. The coloured ones are few and faded, and give the appearance of a fog bathing the scenes. The black-and-whites have preserved better, though a few are stained purple where the chemicals wore off. The edges are crinkled or straight, the corners all worn out and blunt, what do I do with these printed images from another life? There's one, however (but this one I looked for), that stands out, cries out to be admired: a beautiful, fair-complexioned girl with one choti—a thick braid—falling in front across one shoulder; a sweet, partially lit smile hovers on the edge between shy introspection and the flash of boldness that made her pose for the camera, the dupatta fallen casually behind the neck. The mouth is open, captured in a moment of surprise, a glint of teeth just visible, the eyes aglow. The photographer has caught her leaning diagonally across the frame, Indian-actress fashion. At the bottom it's signed in Urdu, which the neighbour's father has read for me, and says, "To Madhu, from your Khatija; with love." *Pyaar se.* What kind of love?

Mother's diary I found in one of her drawers, the locked one containing her delicates and a few items of jewellery. It is a girl's book, yellow with little red flowers, a deep red silk ribbon tying it across. The ribbon is still pretty, carries a shine after all these years, but the yellow of the cover is faded and stained. Good thing I got to it first; no telling what Mohan would have done with it; or, worse still, his wife Anita. Now I can peep into Mother's past, her mind; find out what she was like as a person, besides a mother. I think I owe her that. Her life had an intensity the extent of which I could never have guessed.

A match is in progress outside on the cricket grounds; periodically there comes a roar from the crowds—a wicket taken, or a six-run hit. I was never much interested in the game, so maddeningly slow, and am even less so since I left here, but it is surprising how much of it I absorbed unconsciously as a child. The house fetched a good fifty thousand more, I gather, for the attraction of this cricket vantage point. I remember afternoons when the four of us would have tea in the balcony on a Sunday, watching the last overs of a match played out as the sun set in the distance. Because this is a defence colony, many memories of my childhood are of the military and patriotic sort: marching behind a band on Republic Day; drilling with other children, mock rifles in hand, to prepare for the day when we would be needed for the defence of the nation; the anxiety during two wars, the speeches and patriotic songs, followed by immense relief—as though there were any doubt we would win—and distribution of sweets. The enemy, always Pakistan, the sister nation less than twenty miles away, once a part of this country.

I look at the photo, then at the diary. Then at the photo. With love, from your Khatija. What kind of love? I know the story, but not in these exact—these pained—words.

MADHU

Amritsar, Punjab
April 22, 1947

Dear Khatija—

Something evil is pounding my heart with a pestle, it hurts so, I cannot breathe and I dare not open my eyes to the darkness. There is the smell of burning in the night air and the ugly beastly stench of blood and corpses—Hé Rabba!—can it be true, but my mind conjures these gory pictures from all I heard being said today. This morning, a few hours after you left, another death train arrived, with laashes from Lahore, mutilated bodies, amputated children, missing girls. What happened, my darling, my loving loving Khatija, my friend, I want to hold you in my arms and cry with you, and rock you—do you remember the way we cried each other to sleep when my brother Om died? Save for one wail, my love, this terrible night is quiet, the muezzin has not called and I miss his voice, and I miss the clatter of your front door shutting and your father's keys jangling as he walks to your mosque in the next alley an hour before dawn breaks. Have our gods declared war, Khatija, has Shivji locked horns with mighty Allah, for this dark cloud upon us is no work of mere human hands, this is the Mahabharata of the gods, where cousin flays cousin and hundreds and thousands lie dead—but then why the wrath unleashed upon us women, Khati, and why the innocent children?

*

Pyari pyari Khatija, I knew exactly how frightened you were last night. Believe me, my heart beat in step with every beat of yours as those goonda-log stood outside your doors holding flaming torches ready to burn and kill. Khatija! . . . How fortunate my Bau-ji convinced your obstinate old man to let all of you be locked in from the outside—"Anand Lal, your life is in my hands, don't I know, but trust me for God's sake I won't sell you and yours." And when the goons came and stood outside, shouting rape and murder, and all you twelve people on the other side, half of you women, do you know what agonies I suffered, what promises I made to the Lord? Shall I tell you how many oceans I wept? Then my Bau-ji pushed past granny and Bi-ji and said to them from the window, "Preserve my property, he owed me a lot, that haram-zada Turk!"

"Have they gone?—where?"

"Yes, to Lahore, the bastards, where else?"

And all the while I whispered, O Rabba, Ya Ali, Ya Ali. . . . Do you remember how we sang together in your mosque? And how on dussehra we went to mandir together? Are we different, then, Khati? Your father Anand Lal was also "Hassam" but he was Bhishm Mamu's cousin . . . and your mother Durga was also "Fatima" . . . it is true madness, this difference among people. I don't understand it. I am not educated, but I know it is wrong. There should be no difference between people.

Pyari, are you living or dead now, can you see me? May God preserve you on your journey to Bombay, may you see all the big film stars and may He make you one of them! Lord preserve Anand Chacha and Durga Chachi and little Kuntu and Jahan Bibi and Sheru and Kassam and Noorali and Naseem Banu and Jalalu and my pyari pyari Khatija. . . .

~

April 25, 1947

Pyari . . .

Quickly I must confess before shame makes me forget and bury this sin. I confess that for a moment, for the briefest little pul of time, I felt relief you'd be gone, before grief overtook me again. You know I was always a little jealous of you, Khati, tall and slim and fair, and I short and plump. There, judge me as you will. Remember that day how we spied on your brother Kassam trying on his hat in front of the mirror and strutting about like an English Sahab! I always thought I would marry him. . . . And that afternoon when your Bau-ji hurried inside from the shop, we were sitting on the bed with your mother and laughing, and he told us to leave the room and closed the door . . . and we heard him speaking inside and his voice became soft, and her exclaiming, and whispers and strange sounds. How we blushed. And you said, I so much want to give my milk to someone, and I said, Come, I will be your baby. I feel like that now.

So many memories come back. We were together all our lives. Now suddenly a wall has fallen between us and there is no door or window to look through . . . no sound even, so one may hear and be reassured. Where are you? . . .

This street of smithies is back to normal, but for your home which stands padlocked, silent. It has not seen such solitude in a hundred years, it has never looked so sad; if it could weep, it would. A window upstairs is broken, there are things written on the wall. Someone's left the remains of a mango outside. It can say nothing. It will now be allocated to a refugee family from the other side. The Darbar Sahab is full of refugees and at night we hear the singing of the holy kirtans. Chandra Kaka has visitors who've come from Rawalpindi. They came by train and partly by foot. The man's name is Om Prakash-ji and his wife died on the road. There are two sons, Ramu and Balraj, and a girl Lata who is dying. Her hip is broken and she passes blood all the time. They took her shame on the road, she was tortured repeatedly . . . the story is so terrible, I shudder, and thank God for having saved me, for not making us leave our home.

Will I see you again, my friend? Will you send me a note from Bombay, will you even recognize me when you've become another Noorjehan or Suraiya and the world falls at your feet? Go on, become a heroine of the silver screen, Khati, so that one day I may see you larger than life, with long black hair, and full lips, large black eyes and long eyelashes . . . in the arms of a Prithviraj . . . and how ek-dum thrilled I would be!

~

May 21, 1947

Dear Khatija,

A chitthi arrived, at someone or other's house from someone else who was on the train with you all, that you arrived in Bombay, safe. So I know you are alive—Hé

Rabba, what fears and nightmares have I carried inside me!—and I only await a chitthi from you. Now it seems as if you have simply moved town, though I know you all took only what you could carry and left your life's possessions behind. The door to your place was opened and everything inside taken away. But listen, pyaari, I went inside the house while the police and government people were there and I took your green dupatta with the gold spots; you left it behind and it was your favourite, they let me take it, it still carries your own sweet smell, I would know it anywhere, Khati, in any corner of the world and after a hundred years. I also extracted your notebook in which you would write poems. So I have your writing and your words and your love.

Will you return, Khati, when times are better?

We have a new maid downstairs in the kitchen. Her name is Anasuya. She says she lost her husband and one son in riots last year, and she has no one except her little Pintu, three years old. Bi-ji took pity on her and told her she could sleep in the kitchen. She is a little older than us, Khati, though not more than twenty. Now the strangest thing happened this afternoon after lunch. Anasuya was washing the vessels when she saw little Pintu playing outside the kitchen on the floor. He was naked, as was Bhabhi's little Kishan. As soon as she saw her boy, Anasuya made a dash for him and quickly put his little pyjama back on him which he had dropped off, perhaps to look like his friend. We all stared in amazement, and the girl stared back frightened and with not a word of explanation. Then Bi-ji, Bhabhi, and I looked at each other in silence. We knew.

Can you guess, Khatija? Yes, Anasuya, or whatever her

name is, is a Muslim and she doesn't want little Pintu's circumcision to be seen. But how long can she keep her secret, Khati?

~

May 30, 1947

Oh Khati . . .

I do not wish to live.

Bi-ji has screamed for me, Bau-ji has grumbled outside the door; but I will not get up. For me this dark prison, like Anarkali's tomb.

A most awful discovery.

Yesterday Bi-ji asked me to go clean up Kishore and Raj's room. The maid leaves dust under the beds, so I took a jharu in my hand and went down on my knees to sweep there. No sooner had I stuck in the broom than out rolled a stick. It was a cane for walking, with brass bands going around, and it was covered with dust. Kishore! Raj!—I called as I wiped it with my hands, when Kishore came in and snatched it away from me, almost pulling my arms off. How can I describe what happened next? Such anger in his eyes! My hands were pink from the stains I had uncovered, a strand of grey hair was caught between my fingers. If you speak about this, I will kill you, he said. Such evil words from him! He couldn't have meant them. . . . Now I can't help thinking, my own brother could be a murderer . . . or was he just hiding the stick for someone else? I dare not look into those eyes again.

Now here comes Bi-ji.

~

June 7, 1947

It had to happen and it happened, the most awful thing. First little Pintu went missing. It was four in the afternoon, his mother had not seen him since noon. She went hither and thither in the street asking about Pintu. Where is my Pintu, have you seen my Pintu, arré where is my little boy . . . ? Wasn't he just here, they told her, he was playing, he must be about somewhere. But a mother knows, they say, deep inside her body she knows. She was frantic and she got others worried. She's bad luck only, Bau-ji grumbled to Bi-ji in exasperation, she carries darkness around her wherever she goes. Then finally someone came to the shop and brought news to Bau-ji. Bau-ji came inside to the back, stood for a few moments at the threshold, silently watched us women in the yard, and then he announced, He's been found. Before Bau-ji had quite finished adding, He's dead, Anasuya had rushed to the outside door and uttered such a piercing cry in the alley . . . it cut through my entrails, Khati. Poor Pintu's head was discovered on a pole outside the Darbar Sahab.

Anasuya did not get to see her Pintu again. She sat whimpering in the yard, outside the kitchen, her mind quite gone. The boy's head had been removed by the police and his body found in a ditch. But now everyone knew she was a Muslim. What could we do? She spent the night here, but people came to see Bau-ji in the evening, in the shop, and I could hear the murmurs from where I lay trying to sleep. This morning two policemen and a third man came and demanded to take away Anasuya. Bau-ji said all right, though he was not happy. Anasuya left, pulled roughly by the man who was not a policeman. One of the men in uniform turned and gave first Bau-ji, then the others who had gathered, an obscene grin with his dirty teeth, saying, "We'll take care of her, don't worry."

O Khatija, let this nightmare end.

These three are from your book, Khatija—

Passion burns inside and wastes me away
Know you the object of my inner desire
What gives you that stately glow?

No passion from a thousand lovers
could steal me from my father's home
O innocence my happy playmate
remain a child with me always.

And yet night creeps steadily upon me
smothering everything else in its shadow,
there's only the heart's voice to listen to,
and I don't know anything else in the world.

⁓

July 1, 1947

To the unwary, everything looks normal. Children are playing in the yard, from the empty store down the street comes the sound of boys playing cricket. Really, it is as if nothing untoward happened, except there are holes in our vision where people and sounds are absent. You are absent; your store is locked up and silent. But otherwise business proceeds apace; the sound of hammer on metal tells us so. Two vendors came by today, mountain women, selling apricots and apples. What a treat.

This morning I went to the Darbar Sahab to help with the langar. It had rained earlier and the mist was lifting, and the golden temple shone so brilliantly, it had to make you happy. At the gates two men were polishing the silver doors which you told me your grandfather had worked on. The food was bhindi and baingan, and the halwa had almonds in it. It seems as if we are determined to be happy despite all that has happened.

After we had cut the vegetables and cleaned the rice, and when we sat down for the food and tasted it and praised it, the women of our group suddenly fell silent. Then a girl called Joya started crying, silent tears; and then we all were crying, silently. There was another group of people who were refugees from Pakistan, who had lost much, including family, and they too were silent. After a while one of them came to us, an older woman named Nandini, and comforted us. Mahabharata has happened, she said. The gods have played their game. Now we must go on. We must not insult the temple food. And so we ate.

~

August 17, 1947

We heard Pandit Nehru's speech on the radio. The reception was bad and he spoke in English, but people said it was a most stirring speech. And they have been echoing his words, "The hour of midnight...." We are now, apparently, in independent Hindustan. The English no longer lord over us. But what does the future hold? In spite of the celebrations in the streets and people handing out sweets, there are still reports of violence, and sometimes it feels like a short interlude in the midst of a thunderstorm.

Are you on the other side, Khati—in *Pakistan?* There is no chitthi from you, which must mean that either you are dead, or you are angry with me. But what could I have done, my dearest friend, except grieve, which I have done night and day? Are you my enemy, pyari, because others tell you you are? Must we become what we are told to, my darling, I cannot bear the thought of my heart turning cold toward you, or yours toward mine. Must it all end, Khatija . . . this freedom of our country has quite destroyed me.

~

March 20, 1948

He is a most tender man.

And I see your face among the shadows by the door, next to the almirah, tilted just so, as it always did with mischief, with that puckered smile on your lips, the dimples on your cheeks . . . the stud on your nose aglint in the dawn's first light. . . . At least put that dupatta over your head, in a man's presence!

Are you married, now? . . .

He is not a prince, a nawab, or a raja, and he's not a dashing actor, not a handsome army officer. He's a government babu in the office for resettlement of refugees. The family is from Jullundur, father a teacher; not rich, but his job is good. His name— But I dare not utter it! Let us say the first sound is the same as that of Sita's husband, and it ends in *sh*. That should do, you know that for me he must always be "he." He is not very tall, two finger-widths more than me, but he's very fair, and he has a wide face with pointed chin, large nose, and big ears—a little like an elephant! Go on, laugh all you will at Madhu's choice! Yes, his name does rhyme with Ganesh.

How did the proposal arrive? He came strolling into our alley one day and stopped by at the shop to chat with Bau-ji. He had just been to your mosque, which is now a temporary shelter for refugees, and he asked about the mukhi's house—none other than yours. He had just sat down to eat with Bau-ji and Raj when I returned from college. I was told to fetch water, which I did. I knew I was being watched. Our guest asked Bau-ji what I studied and Bau-ji told me to speak. The guest asked me something in English, which I answered in my broken way! There was one more visit, two weeks later, and then he brought his proposal himself!

They are not rich but are from the high-and-mighty ones. I expect to hear no end from my mother-in-law about this caste difference. Thank God we will not be staying with my in-laws. We have been given a flat opposite the cricket grounds.

Did I tell you he is very educated—he must be, to work as an inspector for the government. He holds a degree from Lahore College and recites Urdu poetry. A man for your own heart! But he's mine.

I would have wanted you to put mehndi with me and sing me those sweet-silly, oh happy! songs of marriage and whisper things in my ear to make me blush. I would have wanted you to be among my family and friends as I went round the fire knotted to him, the pandits reciting the holy shlokas; and as I bade farewell to our alley and all my family and friends, we would have embraced and wept with sorrow and joy; and before I took my first steps away toward my new life, instructed by my father never to look back or come back without my husband by my side, I would have turned and given you one more look and the tightest embrace. I would have liked someone from my old life to share my secrets with, my troubles and joys as a man's wife, ignorant and alone in a new home. Who else but you?

I do not know what the future holds, who knows? On this my first night with him, my lord sleeps peacefully beside me, having satisfied himself as a man does upon his bride. He was tender and loving and not a wild beast. I pray you be as fortunate.

~

Jullundur, Punjab
April 1949

Today I grieve for my dead child ... how the gods tempt us with gifts and then snatch them away; they tease us. I fed him laddoos and butter and fresh milk and halwa, even when I knew he no longer lived inside me. I knew it was a boy from the shape of my belly. My husband's joy knew no bounds. He couldn't wait.

It happened at my in-laws', where I came to give birth. Ganesh-face must have guessed what had befallen, but that witch his mother knew for certain, threw evil eyes and taunts at me, made me cook and toil even in my condition. I truly think she wished me to die with my infant. When I brought him out I insisted on having a look at him, even when they told me that would bring bad luck. My first-born, dead. Strangled himself in the womb. Will I have others, healthy and living? Sometimes I think of that Anasuya and her little Pintu—what lot, a poor mother's. Are these thoughts about you that are evil, has my love for you brought down the Goddess's wrath upon me? No, no. Pray for me Khati that I have one son at least.

LAKSHMI

I never once saw her writing in it;
I never even knew she had it. Fifty years. All I'd seen her write were notes to school when Mohan or I had stayed away due to illness, and shopping lists for Bau-ji. When did she find the time, in her busy life, to pour her heart out into

a book? There was no end to a woman's work; and not much has changed, though we are all educated and modern and know the right words. In the morning she and Bau-ji were up at the crack of dawn, he to shave and do stuff, she to prepare breakfast. She made the parantha herself, the maid relegated to the curry—if that was on the menu—and tea. During lunch, though she sat with us, she was always on edge, one eye turned toward the kitchen, in case she was needed or had to get up to get the maid to bustle up with the chappatis. Bau-ji hated to wait once he was at the table. After school Mother helped us with our lessons. And at night she attended to the needs of Bau-ji. His head, his feet, his frustrations in the bureaucratic workplace.

And yet she herself has no complaint to make, in her private book. Her husband and her family were her duty and joy, so we all like to believe of our mothers. Now I am old enough to know that a woman is more than that; even a traditional woman. Didn't she want to confide something about her marriage to her pyari Khati? Perhaps it was too risky. Perhaps that was why, too, she didn't write as frequently in her book. Bau-ji rarely became angry at home or shouted at her, but once I saw him truly furious. I don't know what happened, but he was suddenly shouting at her, and when I went to look, they were outside their bedroom, and he gave her a slap. I think she had said something about his mother and sisters. A husband's rage is a wife's burden. I have never been able to shake that incident out of my head.

After that last entry of 1949, her letters, or thoughts, to Khatija become occasional. She attempts to fill the pages with household accounts (apparently she tried to save money from her grocery allowance), but not for long. Bau-ji went on official tours for his government department, and she wrote down his itinerary. And there are attempts to write to Khatija that for some reason were aborted; perhaps the children came home from school, or Bau-ji arrived home from work, tired and hungry. Housework always beckoned.

MADHU

Amritsar, Punjab
April 1958

I have two, how many have you?

Tell me why I remember you in the first place, when you have not bothered all these eleven years. Only, I was walking by the Darbar Sahab yesterday and I saw a woman enter and I swore it was you. I thought you must have returned, at least for a visit, now that it is safe.

My Mohan is five and Lakshmi three. Yesterday was Mohan's birthday. I have never been so happy, in so many ages. . . . It is true I have tried to forget you. After that stillborn, for three years I could not hold a child in my womb. The doctors told me my blood was too bitter to nourish a child within me. It is said that bitterness kills bitterness. So I ate karela and grapefruit in quantities, even chewed quinine and Aspirin in secret. I removed your three photos from my album and I put away your green dupatta with the gold spots and your notebook.

(Good thing I did not burn them.) You see, at the temple I vowed to sacrifice my love for you for the blessing of children. What excuse do *you* have for forgetting me? Ganesh-face says that you can't be in Hindustan or you would have contacted me, you must have found yourself in Pakistan. Wherever you are, I hope you are as blessed as I am. When I look at Lakshmi sometimes playing with her dolls, I smile, she reminds me so much of you. You see, even though I vowed to forget you, thoughts of you would steal into my mind like robbers in the night. . . . Mohan was born weak and we constantly worried about him. He would eat little, he could not digest ghee, and put on very little weight. Now he is much better. . . .

But what is this?—I think of me only, what about you, what's happened, where *are* you? Are you, by any chance—married? How many children?

My mother died and Bau-ji retired. The shop is now in the hands of Raj Bhaiya. Kishore has a travel agency at the location where the old Munshi—who was killed during Partition—had his bookstore. He is doing well but we don't meet much. The house next to yours is demolished. Your house has never found a steady occupant, it's always been one family then another, and no one with small children. It always looks forlorn and neglected. Bau-ji says its fate too is demolition. We were by your old mosque the other day, when Ganesh-face and I went with the children to that Victoria Restaurant—since changed to Anand Restaurant. Anand was your father's name, wasn't it? The mosque is now a clothing warehouse. I saw some boys coming down with bales of cotton and my heart broke.

I remembered your brother Kassam, who was so handsome.

No one noticed.

LAKSHMI

When Mohan and I were little, sometimes at bedtime when we worked up a fit of the giggles or started fighting with each other instead of closing our eyes and going to sleep—we shared a room then—Mother would scare us by saying, "If you don't behave, the Pakistani jawans will take you away! Shall I call them? Subedar Khan—over here!" We would get frightened, hide under the bedclothes, trembling but comforted by the knowledge that she was in the room, and finally fall asleep. I don't think I got over those frights. Now I wonder what must have gone through her mind when she said those things. Why say them when they made the sleeping process so terrible. Pakistan was never a threatening spectre for us, except for a week or so during the '65 war: we heard fighter planes in the distance; the flutter of a blackout curtain made the heart leap; every sharp sound could be a bullet. Was she trying to convince herself of her own loyalty, when she made the Pakistanis seem so threatening? Or was it for the benefit of Bau-ji? Or perhaps an old fear lingered from the Partition days when killers ruled the streets, the highways, and the railways?

MADHU

Amritsar
November 1965

Sometimes there's the crack of a gunshot far away in the night, the heart races, and then I sense that he too is awake, beside me, and lying still, waiting. The border is some twenty miles away, all sorts of visions about terrible, violent happenings come to spook the mind. But then the insects begin their clamorous music again, as though a throng of little people were banging on their pots and pans (you taught me this), and nothing has happened to threaten our lives. The fighting has stayed away from us so far. But we hear Ambala was bombed, and Adampur.

War! Our two countries are now at war!

Why do I speak of two countries—is this not your city, Amritsar, couldn't you find my home from your old home in the coppersmiths' alley even blindfolded? The children sing songs of patriotism and bring back flags, the radio plays "vande mataram" no end. The streets are full of soldier-jawans and people say let the war go on a few more days and we will be in Lahore drinking chai in Anarkali Bazaar. I tremble at the thought and I pray it will happen and that I will come over there in Ganesh-face's car and see you there, but please don't hide behind a burqa when it happens. Lahore is Lahore, they say, the unfortunate who has not set eyes on Lahore has not seen the world . . . you were my world, Khati, where are you now?

But your Pakistani army is not full of weaklings either, they are our same Punjabi jawans after all! India may be big, but the Tamils and Malayalis are not going to come over and defend us, Ganesh-face says, and forget about the Bengalis, who would talk away Hindustan! God preserve my Lakshmi and Mohan and also you and yours, from bombs dropped from aeroplanes, from atom bombs, and from marauding soldiers and cutthroats, and let all our shame and modesty be preserved, we who have seen too much in the past.

LAKSHMI

My mother wrote to me regularly when I was in college, first in Chandigarh, then, after I got married, when I was with my husband in Boston. We returned from the United States in 1979 with a baby girl. Not long afterwards Punjab was in the midst of another conflict, this time with the Sikhs demanding an independent homeland. We left to live in Los Angeles. Mother's letters were now longer, reflective and confessional, and I recall wondering at this talent of hers, which had lain hidden for so long, when she seemed to have time for nothing but her family's welfare. Now I know she had perfected that gift on someone else, who had some earlier.

She never forgot about her friend, pyari Khatija, how could she. She did not write in the book because duty always called; and it must often have seemed futile and risky. The girlish habit of confiding in a private book was no longer compelling. I recall her muttering to herself in frustration, as mothers do; but I must be right when I imagine her speaking not just to herself but also to that other, perhaps more intimate presence in her life. And then, after a long respite, unable to resist, Madhu would pick up her pen and book and address her at length; tell her what she told no one else.

MADHU

September 1983

Tell me this was not a dream I dreamt and let me follow you, beckon to me again from that door, say "come," once more . . . "there's a safe place I'll take you to where there's no strife . . . a place far away from madmen whose lust for blood will never be satisfied. . . ." Perhaps your lot turned out better after all, wherever you are. In this Punjab you left behind we yearn for peace once more. Do you know what is happening in your old city? Blood flows again, terror stalks the streets. A wedding party robbed and murdered the other day, a bus stopped and passengers butchered. The army patrols the street, Darbar Sahab, the Golden Temple, is surrounded on all sides. From the terrace of the old house you can see the jawans with guns at the ready pointed at the temple. There are frequent searches in the streets. But in our coppersmiths' alley the soldier-jawans are the heroes. It is said the Golden Temple is full of weapons, but Indira Gandhi is afraid to send the soldiers in. We don't have Sikh friends anymore, there is no trust left. Some of our friends have left the state, and our Lakshmi and Mohan are in America from where they may never return. I will never know my grandchildren.

Iman-se, as you might say, Lakshmi looks just like you—what a twist of fate! And when I saw you in that dream, perhaps it was because I had been staring at her photo and was reminded of you. One day when she was twelve or so, she asked me, Bi-ji, do you know anyone on the other side? Then I told her about you and where you had lived. I don't know for sure if she is on the other side, I said. Then Bi-ji, she told me, Mohan simply can't be allowed to bomb Pakistan, can he? This was at a time when my son had the ambition to become an air force pilot and serve the country. Come over, Ma, she says in her last letter. We've been to America two times now but our heart always yearns for home—and when we are here in beloved Punjab, the crown of Hindustan as our poet Waris Shah said, we live in terror and long to see the grandchildren.

Lakshmi lives in San Francisco, in California, where she is married to an engineer. IIT graduate and working with computers. They have two daughters, Kamala and Indira, six and four years old. Our son Mohan lives in Dallas. He is a professor of English. He is married to an American and has one son, Varun. Perhaps you have seen Dallas on television, in that show that goes by that name. When you see it, please think of me.

~

May 1991

Ah happiness, laughter! I weep tears of joy. How can I explain, who would understand? I catch myself singing!

Finally Ganesh-face said, Mohan's mother, you were not as happy even at your son's wedding!

She looks not the least bit like you, yet your light was shining in her eyes! I could see you in her face. I weep as I think of you, dear Khatija—you didn't write, you didn't come, but finally you sent this lovely angel to bring us together again! O the glory of the gods! O Lord, can this be true, I whisper, that I held *her* flesh and blood in my arms—let her be my daughter, Khati. I am asking this of you, and I have written to her father, your brother.

All this time, for tens of years, you were right next door, in Lahore! I could have come to you on ox cart or train or car, the skies that brought you rain showered on us also, and daily we saw the same moon smiling upon us here as it did on you there . . . every day we could hear Lahore on radio and see its wonderful shairs reciting their Urdu ghazals on television. I don't have your address, Khati—the girl didn't have it with her and she had no idea anyone such as I existed, who knew her grandfather's family so closely and was attached to her phupi since childhood! And let me tell you this, Khati, the girl also wept—why would she cry, she who was not even born in this country? Because of the cloud of grief that hangs over us.

In a few months I will go to California and I will write to you from there and I will telephone you also. A crow can fly from your place to mine, yet we could not shout to each other across the border. This is what's become of us who would spend nights huddled in bed together exchanging secrets and dreams.

FATIMA

Toronto
3 April 1992

Dear Lakshmi,

It was so good to speak to you on the phone and also
to your mother. She did sound rather dispirited com-
pared to when I saw her last year. I was sorry to learn
your father passed away—that must have been quite a
blow to her. He seemed so gentle and devoted to her
when I met them.

Our meeting was the most heart-wrenching and of
course at the same time a happy occasion. And what a
fortunate one! One reads so much about the Partition of
India, and yet to come face to face with it, in one's own
life and so close! In a strange way that I cannot quite
explain, I too feel a victim of the Partition.

My father never went back to Amritsar, though he visited India many times, from East Africa, where I was
born. But a few years ago Dad (whom I never thought of
as nostalgic) got it into him that he wanted a photograph
of the house he was born in, or even of the site, in case
the house had been destroyed. When a certain Sikh professor from Guru Nanak University came to Toronto on
a lecture tour, Dad went to meet him and asked him if
upon his return to Amritsar he could take a photo of the
old house or neighbourhood and send it to him. The professor duly did so—the house stood there, but in ruins.
Then last year when I told my father I was planning to
visit his hometown with my family during our trip to

India, he gave me Professor Hardev's name and address. The rest you know. We visited the coppersmiths' alley in the old city (which is such a maze of narrow streets, we couldn't have found our way inside without our guide Professor Hardev); we saw my grandfather's house, then stopped to inquire at the shop across the street, which turned out to belong to your uncle! We had tea at his house and telephoned your mother, who we learned from your uncle had been my aunt Khati's dearest friend as a child. When I spoke to your mum on the phone, we both broke down. How cruel, fate—and yet surely a touch of kindness there? I had a feeling that I was reaching out to a long-lost and very dear relation; of course your mother broke down first, but still. Not only had I not met her yet, I had not (and have not) met my aunt (though I had heard about her).

Later my family and I visited Jallianwala Bagh (the site of the 1919 massacre and a walking distance from my grandfather's old home) which, with bullet holes and all, impressed my son no end and turned him into an ardent anti-imperialist; and we went to the Darbar Sahab, or Golden Temple, with its memories of a more recent bloodshed. The Temple is visible from my grandfather's house, from the terrace, over all the neighbouring houses. Then, in the afternoon, we went to see your parents.

I cannot forget how she (your mum) cupped my face in her hands and stared at me. She recalled everyone in my father's family and asked about them. And how she laughed when I told her my Khati Phupi has twelve children!

Khati Phupi is at present in Dubai with one of her

numerous children. Did your mum get to speak to her on the phone? Perhaps we can get the two ladies to meet when Khati Phupi goes to Phoenix to see her daughter (who is a doctor).

I will call your mother before she leaves. And now that the two of us have established contact, we should remain in touch. Please accept my heartfelt best wishes for you and your family.

Yours sincerely,

Fatima

LAKSHMI

San Francisco

5 August 1992

Dear Fatima:

Yes, they met finally. It was not what one would expect—but what *can* we expect! As if such reunions happened every day!

We did not know that your Khatija Phupi was recovering from an eye operation. She stayed two nights, at our place—we insisted. But her son Latif had come with his family and put up in a hotel.

And now the details.

Khatija was dropped off at the door by Latif, who said he would stay longer when he came to pick his mother up. She was big—wide and tall—and wore a light cardigan over the shalwar kameez. She walked slowly, has problems with her knees and is contemplating surgery. I simply couldn't help staring at her as she came, you see I had heard about her even as a child. I had always imagined her as beautiful as a screen actress, and what I was seeing now was a much older, yet very striking, woman. Her face had the kind of irritated, pained look that the elderly tend to have, through which she gave a shy, uncertain smile, and her eyes quickly swept through the room. My mother was in the kitchen and before I called out she made her entrance. Briefly the two women stood and watched each other across the distance, then without a word uttered they started walking toward each other—slowly at first, then in a hurry. They embraced, quietly, wiped tears from their eyes—but not too many. They sat down on a couch, next to each other. Khatija was the first to speak. "You look well," she said. "But you were the pretty one."

"How are you, Khati?" my mother asked, in a tremulous voice.

"Almost blind in one eye, but inshallah another operation has been scheduled."

They spoke quietly, one voice softer than the other; quite a contrast, the two of them, as they must always have been. I kept out of their way for some time, making the tea and so on, and fetching the kids from school. It was the strangest feeling for me—I wished I could read their minds. In that first hour they spoke only of their lives *now*—like two strangers—and then there would be some "inside" remark like "you would always . . ." or "like that Shahniji's son. . . ."

Over the next two days they spoke a little about the past, about their experiences since they parted that morning in

Amritsar. Khati and her family arrived in Bombay with nothing—their train had been so crowded, they had to give away the only suitcase they had between them, to be placed in storage and make room for one more passenger, and they never saw it again. Fortunately they knew people in Bombay. In August 1947 they took a ship to Karachi. Your father was already in East Africa, having left two years before. The following year Khati was given in marriage to a man from Lahore. Her husband, Ashfaq, was a dealer in carpets, which is what Latif Bhai does in Phoenix.

What else? They were solicitous about each other, spoke (boasted!) about their children, exchanged notes on their medications—but they could not completely break out of that formality. It's been forty-five years since they last saw each other! Toward the end, though, there was one precious moment of closeness, and I'll tell you about it. On the last day, when they sat down cross-legged on my kitchen floor to sort out and label my daals, Khati Phupi pointed and said to Mother, "Your right knee always came higher than your left when you sat—and your Bi-ji would scold you."

Mother broke into a giggle and Khati Phupi smiled. But I could also see the tears in my mother's eyes, immediately after that; Khati Phupi must have seen them too. She's a tough woman, Fatima, there's no telling what she's been through. She has a dry sense of humour, and she does not easily show her emotion. That afternoon it was time for her to go. Did I detect a tremor in her voice as she bid my mother goodbye? They parted knowing they'll probably never see each other again.

Mother was depressed after that.

Two weeks later your uncle Kassam came from

Vancouver with his wife and he was a lot of fun. He joked around and made fun of Mother, calling her "Madhu Didi," and she laughed a lot.

Now Mother is back in Amritsar. She is going to be lonely there, but she insisted. Anyway, she has an open ticket to come here whenever she feels like it.

Let's stay in touch, Fatima. Do come to SF and bring your family. My husband goes to Montreal on business sometimes—maybe one of these days we'll all come together. I've heard so much about Toronto.

My regards to you and your family.

Yours with affection,

Lakshmi

MADHU

Amritsar, Punjab
August 1992

You did not recognize that dupatta I wore, it was yours from so many years ago, but how could you have remembered? I felt like a tortoise. And you? How could we come out from under the weight of fifty years of life and be like we were, relate like we used to?

I sensed a hurt in you, dear, I can't tell where from. But I would have broken through that sternness, Khati, found that soft inside, given time. But now we belong to others, and you to many more than I.

But I will keep your book, I will not return it. How could it have the same value to you as it does to me?

This is from the book—

O my friend, to whom shall I tell the
story of my loss,
My lover travels far and wide
and I'm afraid will not return.

It's an old doha you used to sing.

She, with Bill and George

The tree. Yes it always began
with the tree, her memory of that time, that place—a
large, knotty jacaranda in bloom, purple bell flowers
drooping down from its branches. She was sitting under
its shade rather self-consciously one Saturday morning,
on a thin carpet of fallen flowers, a diary in her lap, trying to write her thoughts down. She was in her National
Service uniform, baggy khaki pants and matching tunic,

and the unwieldy black boots. Dreamy, that's what she was, her feet partly pulled up, occasionally gazing up at the branches, the blue sky, for inspiration. And alone, away from friends, family, community—and Shamshu—in the wilderness outside the small town of Mbeya in the southern highlands where she had been assigned to teach a school. It was a cool region of the country; fruits were abundant—peaches, plums, and apples—the people were nice; sometimes she was terribly lonely, but she also relished being alone, as at times like these.

There came a soft scratch of feet behind her and then the voice: "Eating the air?—isn't that what you say?"

She turned her head, threw an eye sideways up at Bill. He was an American: typical, she liked to think, tall and stringy, casual, too friendly. He wore shredded jeans and a blue shirt tucked in, in accordance with an admonition from the principal, who himself always wore the party shirt suit. Bill Songa, a maths teacher from the Peace Corps; such a funny name. She had told him once that in her language to go out for a breath of fresh air became translated as "to go and eat some air." They were a threesome, she, Bill Songa, and George Kasore, all strangers to these parts. George was a Masai and as tall as Bill. Unlike the American, he always wore clean and pressed printed shirts and dark pants. The two played basketball, always on opposite sides, with teams consisting of a horde of adulatory boys. She envied them their popularity. And they both liked her, this Indian girl a full head shorter than them, shy and reserved.

"Hi!" she said to him. "And what are you up to?"

Nothing, as she well knew, he had come to kill time before the lunch gong.

He smiled. "George and I are going into town today, would you like to come?"

Bill had got himself an ancient German car, a DKW, so he could go and paint the town red, as he jokingly put it. One Friday she had taken a ride with him and George so she could go to mosque in Mbeya; on their way back she realized that they'd had a few beers. She found the smell a little revolting. The next time, they promised, they would simply go with her to a restaurant for chai and samosas. There had not yet been a next time.

"No thanks," she replied.

"You afraid your fiancé will not approve?" he asked. She nodded and giggled. "Are you really engaged, Farida, or are you putting us on?"

"Really. His name is Shamshu, as I've told you before. And he's a teacher in Dar."

Bill was now leaning back against her tree. It was called "her" tree because practically everyone in the school had come to know that it was her favourite spot. When the gong sounded, they walked to the dining hall together. George joined them at the tables. Lunch was maizemeal and red beans, another reason to go and eat something decent in the town, come weekend. But she had in her room enough supplies of chevdo and gathiya, Indian savouries, to placate taste buds clamouring for spices.

After lunch she agreed to go with the two guys for a walk. The route was a trail through bush and trees and over a brook into a nearby village. On the way they passed folk who, as always, broke into wide but kindly smiles at seeing an Indian girl in an army uniform. A little boy threw her a salute, then with a few others followed behind in a mock march. At the village was a stall whose owner was always ready to make tea for them, even after he had put his fire out.

As they returned, she sang for the two men some of the National Service songs she had learned at her military camp earlier that year. One of them went,

Niko mlimani na Landa
na ngojea Pijo kupanda.

I'm up the hill in my Land Rover
and waiting for the Peugeot to come over.

It then exhorted youth to tighten their belts and serve the nation. Rain fell, brisk and thin as a curtain, and they scampered through the forest back to the school. By the time they arrived the sun was out and beaming through the clouds. The air was humid. The leaves looked new.

A typical Saturday in her life, then, a long time ago. Simple, spare, but in a pure, almost mystical sense. Perhaps that was the way of childhood—pure and mystical—seen from afar. And perhaps, too, it was a composite Saturday she recalled, of similarly wonderful weekend days. But the purity couldn't last, could it?

On one of their walks, when they had strayed onto a vehicle track running perpendicular to their usual route, an army Land Rover passed them, then stopped abruptly. An officer, sitting next to the driver, shouted, "You, come here!" They all started obediently toward the vehicle. As they approached, the officer snapped, "You!" at Farida. Trembling she went up to him and saluted, and he asked her, "Where is your belt, soldier?" She was actually wearing a civilian belt and he had noticed that. She mumbled that she had lost it, and he told her to find a replacement.

"I didn't know there was an army camp here," she said nervously, watching the Land Rover head off.

"Guerrillas? . . ." said Bill.

"You mean . . . training them for Mozambique and South Africa. . . ."

George said, "Hmm."

A week later an army belt was delivered to the principal's office. Farida was delighted; she was appreciated.

In the evenings she would read. The school library was good, and Bill had a constant supply of American paperbacks that he lent her. One day he gave her a copy of Jacqueline Susann's *The Love Machine* with a glint in his eye. She did not proceed further than the description on the back cover, returning it with a meaningful "Thank you."

~

Toronto
November 6, 1999

Dear Bill,

I don't know why I am writing this letter to you . . . I simply had this overwhelming compulsion to do something unusual, courageous, and . . . foolish? I felt like grabbing a fistful of my life that's so rapidly passed away, relive clearly those years . . . no, not quite like that, but a compulsion to touch the past again! Do you know what I mean? If you reply to this letter, then I'll know that yes, those times we spent together at St. Andrew's were real; and perhaps we can remind ourselves of them!

I have decided to write to you at your parents' address, which I've remembered after all these years ("40 Fairmount Ave, Haverstock, NY 10929," just like that, pat), hoping that somehow someone, whoever lives there now, will forward the letter to you. I wish I could do the same with George, but I don't have a clue where to write to him. Do you? Have I lost him completely?

I pray that you at least are there and together we can hunt him down!

Affectionately,
Farida.

~

Cleveland
11 November 1999

Dear Farida:

Thank you. Ahsante. I'd like to paint that across the sky in mile-high red letters so you could see it from where you are in Toronto. You don't know what your letter has meant to me. And yes, those times we spent together were real, how often have I recalled them! I have hundreds of slides from back then but nobody to show them to! I live quite alone now. After I returned from Tanzania, I went to grad school for a year, then dropped out, and worked as travel agent, insurance broker, and finally pharmaceutical salesman. I was married and have two children, both in college now.

I have a confession to make. Ten years ago I did return to Tanzania and met George. He had had quite a career. He had published a novel, not very successful, worked as a headmaster at a school in Arusha, and been a diplomat in Moscow, Stockholm, and Washington DC! He was quite touched to see me. It was the last thing he expected! We both remembered you with affection. He accompanied me and the kids to the game parks but was bored, and I'm sorry to say drank a bit too much. He didn't seem happy. He had fallen out of favour with the government and was awaiting some assignment overseas. I don't know where he is now.

I'm sending this to your office as you requested. Is there any chance we could meet? Cleveland is not far away from where you are. Tell me about yourself.

Love,

Bill.

~

You're still there! And George, where is he? I can find out, if I wanted to, I've got connections that you don't. We Indians exist in networks, don't you know that! You didn't send a photo, but then I didn't either, did I . . . are you fatter now, or still as bony and angular as you were then . . . striding through the bushes, you were quite a walker. We had a theory about you, George and I—did you know that? We *suspected* you!

*

For instance when she had begun, to their joy, taking the occasional ride with her two friends to go and visit the town—

She had been "adopted" by a family there called the Bhanjis; she was royalty when she visited them, which was a bit embarrassing for her. But to them it was their duty to look after a single girl sent by an insensitive government to work in the countryside. They cooked the best food for her, gave her a comfortable bed to lie on, had her laundry done, and in the evening they took her to the local community mosque. The next day, Sunday, they dropped her off back at St. Andrew's. Her fiancé Shamshu could also call her at the Bhanjis or leave messages. The small-town life was enchanting in its way; everybody knew everybody else, you could walk down the street and stop for a chat at half a dozen places. One day when she went to buy her last-minute supplies at a local shop, the man there mentioned that the American teacher telephoned Nairobi from his shop every time he came to Mbeya. The next day when she said to Bill, "I didn't know you had close friends in Nairobi," he gave a start, and she explained, "Oh, that Karmali Masa said you called Nairobi every time you go to Mbeya." Bill said he had a cousin in Nairobi. Then there was this guy who came to visit Bill from Dar and wore rather stylish safari clothes. He said he knew Bill from back in college, but Bill had said he had met him first in Ghana.

"Do you think . . ." she said to George (they were sitting under her tree).

"What?"

"Could Bill be a spy, is that possible, you think?"

"Like James Bond."

He looked amused and she laughed, "Not quite, but. . . ."

"He could be supplying information, I think Americans would be asked to do that by their government."

They looked knowingly at each other. Bill was their friend, they saw no harm in him. And they never let on their suspicion. And he, Bill, did he think them simple, innocent, and naive? After all, the Dar papers occasionally did have stories about all sorts of agents: Americans, Chinese, Russians. She and George, the locals, on the other hand saw Bill sometimes as the genial and nice but quite naive American.

You might have thought that it was to Bill that she would have been attracted: his composure, his confidence, his authority, and he was *American*. But it was George who intrigued her like . . . something dangerous and attractive. Who had heard of an Asian girl attracted to a black man? It was absolutely unthinkable, not possible. Yet when they were together (Bill not around), there seemed to be an electricity around George, it was like being in a charged "field" (a concept which Bill had explained to her). Between them they laughed, yes, but there was more to him and she was aware of that.

The teachers lived in a small block of flats apart from the student dormitories. A red-earth flagstoned path led to the teachers' quarters from the school compound. One afternoon while returning from lunch with George, he invited her for tea in his flat, which came before hers. It was on the ground floor. Bill was behind them and she assumed he too was invited; she even waved at him to indicate so. But Bill went on and she found herself alone with George. It didn't bother her much, just that she didn't want other teachers to form the wrong impression. It was there that, when she finished her tea and put down the cup and saucer, he declared his feelings; but he prefaced his speech awkwardly with "My dear—" so that, startled, she gave a little giggle, before he tumbled out with, "I love you, Farida."

Just that. The simple truth. "But, but—" She was confused, she turned red (she must have). Total shock. Like when you're a child and fall flat on your stomach and get up and don't know where you are, why the tears are falling. Not angry, or offended, she realized, after a minute's silence; and not too surprised: *what* he said was not what she reacted against as much as the fact that he said it, articulated it. He came and sat beside her, took both her hands in his. "George," she said primly, pulling her hands away, "you know very well that I am engaged." Besides religion and all the other differences . . . she must be as pink as a bougainvillea flower. Not for an instant did it occur to her that she didn't care for him, that he was repulsive, presumptuous. He sensed something receptive in her and put his arms around her, and he kissed her. She would recall the fragrant soap on him, his towering height bending over her, his rough and wet mouth. She could be aroused as she had discovered during her secret meetings with Shamshu back home in Dar. "No"—she pulled herself away, and she could see that he could barely control himself from going further than that kiss. But he desisted and went to sit across from her on a chair. She arranged her hair and clothes, got up and went out.

There was an impassioned exchange between them again a few days later, while on their way to the school one afternoon, he having caught up with her from behind, when she explained patiently to him that she was engaged, committed to this guy she had known for the past so many years.

"But you don't say that you love him—" he said pointedly.

"I do love him, I don't have to tell you that."

"And you have no feelings for me whatsoever?"

"Not those kind . . . look, I do love you but in my own way. . . ."

"Along with the rest of the world. What do you think, I'm a creature of some sort you can have love for, or some plant perhaps—"

"George, why do you have to spoil everything—"

"You mean my being black has nothing to do with it?"

"No." But of course there was that, too, except she didn't know what sort of difference it made. She was, conveniently, engaged.

"If you only knew how *much* I love you, Farida. No one will—no one *dare*—ever love you as much."

They remained friends. The electricity was there between them. She cared for him, very much, would have loved to get to know him better. He remained passionately in love with her.

Her fiancé came on a visit. Shamshu stayed with her, which was awkward since they were not yet married. He didn't see much of George but saw quite a bit of Bill, who was always around with jokes, and questions, and suggestions—the friendly American whose height he found rather intimidating, and whose closeness with Farida made him not a little jealous. And Bill was partly the reason why Shamshu, sounding somewhat awkward and furtive, told her, "Why not quit work now, how long can we go on like this, let's get married quickly and apply to go to Canada." Farida said, "Yes, let's." There was no point in prolonging the present state of affairs. She spoke to her parents over the phone from Mbeya about this new plan, and they approved. They were only too anxious to see her settled, a single girl so far away from family.

She was somewhat stoic in her goodbyes; she hadn't realized how cut up she would feel, in a part of her, at leaving so suddenly. She might never see Bill again. But they promised to write. George found out she was going, but not from her; she had not had an opportunity to tell him, and he'd been keeping away. He met her in a corridor once, briefly, and said, "I understand you're leaving us." "Yes," she said, mouth agape as though about to add something, but what? "Good luck," he said. But the day she left—it was lunch break—saying "One moment" to Shamshu as they were about to board the car, she ran to George's flat, knocked, went in, and said: "I've come to say goodbye." He had stood up from the sofa, a magazine in his hand. "Goodbye," he said. "I wish you a happy life." "You too . . ." she said, choking, and left.

No promise to write, to keep in touch; perhaps she should have given him her address. But for what. How could she write to him?

~

Did I ask myself what exactly I felt for him ... what he had asked me to risk, what that would have entailed ... did I ever wonder afterwards whether I simply played it safe, was unwilling to scorch myself in a passion ... that perhaps my decision was to live not fully but longer? How easily I decided to forget him, them both. How easily we cast aside, walk away from voices, from love, from friendship, from parts of our lives ... and how desperately we try to grasp them when they are beyond reach. George, you'd never have been happy, I knew that. Perhaps it was that unhappiness I shrank from. But no, I just didn't have it in me simply to fly away, the other way, from my flock, they were my golden cage, my security ... my sanity.

~

Cleveland
3 September 2000

Dear Farida:
Thank you for your letter. It was certainly a long time coming. I understand—or I think I do. I suspected, you see. Am I talking out of line here? I don't mind saying that your letter broke me up completely. I am extremely sorry, I only wish *I had stayed in touch*, with you, with him. It took you to seek me out, when I could have done the same, earlier. And it took you to find out about him. What a tragic fate. We can make excuses, but for my part there are none I will accept from myself. I was callous and forgetful, thinking life goes on. It doesn't, at some point, does it?

Let's keep staying in touch, dear Farida, for our sakes and also his. God, how I miss him now.
With love from,
Bill.

~

A young African with a thin face, in what we used to call a Kaunda suit, stares from a faded picture on the faded cover of a long out-of-print book—the orange, black, and white cover of the AWS literature series that we used to read during those days at school. It was left on an end table, deliberately, by my wife, partly I think to test whether I recall the name of the author, George Kasore. I do, of course, and recall meeting him briefly during that visit when I brought her back home, to marry me and move her far away. I did not think much about him, but those were the days. His existence was outside of my domain. Three letters from Bill Songa I also found, conspicuously, on top of the book. Offerings to my curiosity, for me to discover a part of her life, as I promise myself I will.

Farida

Some evenings we find our-
selves sitting together in the living room, caught in a
space, a moment, a span that lies between the unspoken
intimacy and closeness of years spent together and our
private worlds that have grown simultaneously and
inevitably inside us; sitting diagonally across from each
other, which is how we've grown accustomed to viewing
each other, after a long day, a middle-aged couple well

into a good joint innings, with memories and thoughts that erupt into gentle but sudden revelations we make about ourselves to each other; she reading a book or knitting, a new hobby undertaken with an almost biological urge as if an assertion of womanhood or motherhood; and I with the business section of the paper, or something else to cast an idle eye upon. And then I begin to drift, get drawn into myself, and I pick up this: my notebook and pencil; and she, having observed me withdraw with a concerned look toward her, makes a small try to keep me.

"You do embellish," she says with a smile.

"I don't embellish," I defend myself. "I know the stories, and I know the characters—surely I can fill in?"

"You were always good at adding mirchi masala," she insists, bringing in the past, knitting it, I imagine, intently into that sweater.

We go back a long way together, she knows things about me I've forgotten.

The earliest I imagine us together is in those sunny days of Tom Jones's "Green, Green Grass of Home," and of "Guantanamera," and the heyday of the Beatles. Yes, those were our days. I had in my keeping for some reason the key to a storage room in our mosque, and on those bright musical Sunday mornings, the air fragrant with the aromas of sizzling spices in buttery ghee, we would meet on the quiet in the compound of that mosque and go to that room, which contained heaps of rolled-up carpets on which we would sit and share passionately of our intimacies, holding on tremblingly to our virginities. How terribly sweet were those days, how thrilling and anxious our pubescence, how the future loomed before us in its vastness, its abundance—all those possibilities! We gave up—or let's say we lost—an idyllic, naive existence as a people in a small city, in a small country, far from the bustling anxiety and screech and snarl of modernity. That loss was inevitable, obviously; but perhaps not the violence with which it happened—I don't mean of the physical sort, though there was some of that too, but the sudden and total upheaval in our ways and the scenery around us, the lack of gradualness. But, as we sit here musing on an evening, Farida and I—the kids out of the house, one grown up and gone for good, the other out somewhere with friends—we know we've not done badly at all, that our upheaval pales beside those of Somalia and Ethiopia, South Africa and Bosnia. Who would complain? And this place we arrived at, three decades ago now, also went through its upheaval because of so many like us who had come to settle here. But it changed, this city of ours, from a scrubbed, antiseptic piece of concrete—so it seemed to us—into the exciting and exotic metropolis that it now is.

In those early days some twenty-five of us would meet in a small room on the lower level of Flemingdon Park Mall; that room was our mosque, and the locals had not seen anything like it. Come rain or shine, hail or snow, it would open for prayers, and the chorus of singing or chanting or the single voice raised in announcement or leading a prayer, echoed through the corridor, wafted up the open staircase to the floor above. Fortunately for everyone, it was evening, when few shoppers were around, or early in the morning, when there was not a soul in the building except a watchman. I remember being followed closely by a police car at four in the morning once, on my way to prayers. I was on foot and alone, and I would look behind me nervously, unsure what I should expect or do. It was January and biting cold. Finally the car stopped and the cop inside asked me to get in and requested my identification. I gave him my passport, informed him where I was going. "I'll take you there," he said. He was rather young. It turned out I was not the only one so favoured by his attention. We gave him the name "Bill." Many times he would watch us from the parking lot of the mall or from the doughnut store as we emerged shortly after five. How does he recall those encounters, I wonder? And what was his real name? Ashiq, our son, was one and Mira was yet to be born. Farida and I had married soon after graduating from university, and when Ashiq came we applied to go to Canada.

The university campus in Dar back then was beautiful, I don't know what it's like now. It was located away from the city, on a hill, in luscious surroundings with large ample spaces, and its quiet walking lanes amidst the tropical gardens and shrubbery had been ideal for us to stroll through in the evenings and hold hands and murmur endearments and make plans for ourselves. Outside of these moments alone there was little privacy in our lives; rooms were shared and friends whom we'd known most of our lives, as neighbours and community members, were all around. Weekends we went home. She tells me I was quite the comedian and yarn-spinner then, among our group, and as a major in history quite the reader and intellectual. Sometimes during our walks at night we found a quiet spot behind a tree, ostensibly to sit together in a moment of emotion before we parted but actually for a cuddle and a little lifting of the dress and so on. University had not provided us with a private haven for our mischief, like the one we'd had before in that storage room in the mosque; not that she minded, we were older and she was more conscious of herself. The need for closer intimacy was mine, but I knew if we had a place to ourselves she would relent, if only partially. That was the understanding and trust in our love.

One Sunday night, as we emerged from the dining hall and paused and wondered which direction to turn to for our stroll, she informed me her roommate had stayed home, would return tomorrow. Just that, and the look. We headed, in an ostensibly casual manner, for her room. Once the door closed behind us we fell on each other with a passion. How much I had longed for this moment, there was for the first time a bed with us! And how we strained to preserve what we had, our innocence, not to cross the line. And how much we wanted to do just that, break through those bounds into a new state which we were sure would leave us intact. Past those first stages of squeezing and holding, the weighty awkwardness of inexperienced bodies, the touching of intimacies and putting-just-the-tip-there, I could hardly contain myself, I was in and we were one. Can there be any greater pleasure than that first time in frightened, frantic, and ecstatic love? We lost our virginities and did "it" just that one time but I walked around a proud stud, with my woman beside me.

I see her sitting across from me now and I want to go
and touch her; but if I do I am afraid I will lose my train
of thought. This worries her, my notepad on my lap; and
it worries me, too. Can I control what thoughts, what revelations and stories, what part of myself I put down here?
Can we bear the pain of this scrutiny, this veiled and
treacherous truth?

What an anxious month we passed when she missed
her period that time, following our misdemeanour.
Initially, though, when she told me the news and what it
implied—a child—I find it hard to believe how laugh-
ably naive I was—I felt like an even bigger man,
confirmed: I had planted one, as the vulgar saying went.
Only later, as we continued our stroll that evening, did it
dawn on me what she was fretting about by my side. If
she was truly pregnant, we would become the laughing-
stock among our friends; we would be branded among
some sections of the community as shameless sinners.
Couldn't we have *waited?*—what was the hurry?—the
whole world waited (our elders' pained admonishments).
We would be known and talked about forever. Our wedding would be a hurried, pushed-through, tainted affair,
instead of a full-scale glorious celebration. But first, she
said, allowing a glimmer of hope into our predicament,
her condition had to be confirmed by a doctor—there
was a tiny chance that this was a false alarm and we were
safe after all. But what doctor to trust? An Indian was out
of the question, the story would be out and spreading
within a day. An African doctor could botch the test, or
worse. A European—white—seemed the best choice, for
competence and discretion. But a white doctor was

inconveniently far and probably very expensive. We laugh when we recall that quandary now, what silliness that panicky circumstance led us into. What colonial and racist attitudes we had. I made up a story for my friends who were studying science that our servant at home wanted a pregnancy test done for his sister, and wouldn't it be a good idea to do it ourselves. With chemicals stolen from one of the labs and test tubes and kitchen supplies, a messy and smelly test was performed by me and others on a gas stove at a friend's house; the solution that would reveal my fate, and that of my beloved, had to be kept standing steady for five days, and I left it in a tea cup on my friend's kitchen window with strong reminders to his mother not to empty it into the sink. Which is precisely what a servant ended up doing a couple of days later. Time was running out and I was beginning to appear both guilty and silly with my vague and inconsistent talk of my servant's sister's crisis and the urgency of a test. Finally I took assistance from an African intern, who had the test done at the public hospital, confirmed a negative result, and told Farida to relax and await her next period. My next "deed"—as we called it—with my girl was on our wedding night, with all the huzzahs preceding it, after the wedding reception. Ashiq was born not long after.

That name, Ashiq, has a certain old-worldness to it; it comes from poetry, and it means "lover"—both in the mystical and the worldly sense. A moth that burns itself in the flame of a candle is an ashiq who dies for its love. A few years after we arrived in Canada, his name was predictably corrupted to Ash, which he altered in spelling to Ashe, after the famous black tennis star, who eventually died of AIDS.

One day we received a call from one of Ashe's teachers, a Mr. Turner; a rather nice fellow, soft-spoken. I would like to discuss your son with you, how he's doing and so on. Perhaps he's started slipping up in class, what with the teenage years upon him, we worried, though we were also confident the matter couldn't be serious; we knew our son, our first-born who'd shared that first winter with us in this country, and that dingy apartment on Dufferin where we spent a couple of months before we knew better and moved out. When we sat down before Mr. Turner, he began by saying very positive things about Ashe, which put us at ease. Then he went on to explain to us about the importance of freedoms and human rights, and we listened and wholeheartedly agreed, though not without a trace of irritation; we were educated, perhaps as much as he, we too had been teachers, though briefly, in the country we came from. Observing our impatience, he began to speak of sexual preferences and slowly the point of the interview began to dawn on me; it required the full brunt of the revelation before Farida realized what was being said: Your son is gay. She looked at me as if to say, Something's wrong with my hearing today, or, Is this man crazy?

We've taken it well. We've read books and had discussions with doctors and teachers. It is nothing wrong, it's not perversion. We are convinced. But I must confess to the initial shock, the disappointment. A lifetime's expectations, is what it comes down to; a man sees himself in his son. And a man has hopes for grandchildren, a continuation of the genes. To come upon a deviation from the norm in one's own line, that's the rub. My son will not be a father, a husband; will not have a woman beside him and all that involves: man and woman. Instead, man and man, and whatever they are up to. I cannot erase from my mind all those scenes from long ago when as boys we would make jokes about homosexuality, about those "uncles," the strange, silent and pathetic elderly men with a certain reputation. After the initial shock, Farida took to the idea much more readily. He was always sensitive, she said, and gays are sensitive, they are artists, aren't they? W. H. Auden, and Benjamin Britten, and. . . . And our own Mr. Gregory, the English teacher, he was also a poet, I added. Thus we are comforted. Ashiq was our jewel, is still our jewel. He did not become an artist, some sort of unemployed poet, and that's perhaps as well. He is a geologist in Alberta.

Ashe was extremely moved when he found out we knew, that we had accepted what he was. But you are our son, we told him, and will always be that. Our disappointment, our expectations, we have swallowed, he knows that; and every time he comes to see us, I can tell he still is moved. And every time we meet, we embrace. I am proud of my son, that we had a son. Only, it seems that one day he just rode away into the sunset, into another mode of existence. That's life. One day a friend of Ashe called to invite us to a birthday party in his honour and we went, not knowing what to expect, even what to wear. We went after mosque and so I was in my suit, which was out of place, but Farida in a bright blue sari stood out like a peacock and people simply gaped at her. They were a nice bunch, who met us, all young and mostly men, but it was like being among a group of aliens. And, as I said to my son, "But you guys dress alike and look alike," to which he answered, "Maybe among the younger guys, but there are others . . . I could introduce you to some older guys if you're interested!" It was too soon for that kind of humour. At the party we met Ashe's "partner," Shelly, the guy who had called to invite us.

Now she's got up with a smile and a glance at me, which is a signal that perhaps I should follow, in a while, and I'm left with this, my preoccupation that's beginning to stand between us, though slightly, and the thought of that other preoccupation, the peccadillo I've got myself into, a yearning for someone else that I can't control though I have no desire even to consider letting this one go, this partner of so many years and experiences. And as that other looms at the back of my mind, I wonder about this one: does she guess, does she know? Am I living on borrowed time, is this dual existence so far a gift from her?

About the Author

M.G. Vassanji won a regional Commonwealth Prize for *The Gunny Sack* (1989). He is the author of four other novels: *No New Land* (1991); *The Book of Secrets* (1994), which won the inaugural Giller Prize and the Bressani Prize; *Amriika* (1999); and *The In-Between World of Vikram Lall* (2003), which made Vassanji the first writer to win the Giller Prize a second time. He is also the author of a collection of short stories, *Uhuru Street*. He was awarded the Harbourfront Festival Prize in 1994 in recognition of his achievement in and contribution to the world of letters, and in the same year was chosen as one of twelve Canadians on *Maclean's* Honour Roll. Born in Kenya and raised in Tanzania, M.G. Vassanji attended university in the United States and lives in Toronto.

A Note About the Type

The body of *When She Was Queen* has been set in Janson, a misnamed typeface designed in or about 1690 by Nicholas Kis, a Hungarian in Amsterdam. In 1919 the original matrices became the property of the Stempel Foundry in Frankfurt, Germany. Janson is an old-style book face of excellent clarity and sharpness, featuring concave and splayed serifs, and a marked contrast between thick and thin strokes.

Acknowledgements

Thanks to Lara Hinchberger for her patience; and to Nurjehan, Pankaj, and Charu for reading the manuscript during its various stages.